*helio*graphica

For Betty
a great writer
and friend

Sharon

Slaybells Ring

by

Sharon King-Booker

*helio*graphica

*helio*graphica

For information:
Heliographica
2261 Market St., #504
San Francisco, CA 94114

www.heliographica.com

Library of Congress Control Number: 2004112463
ISBN 1-933037-26-1

Printed in the United States of America

DEDICATION

This book is dedicated with gratitude and love to my aunt, Wilda Beyers, who has always been there for me with both love and encouragement. Also to my husband, Thom, who has helped me burn the midnight oil.

PROLOGUE

The axe was raised high, light glistening off its polished surface and refracting off its edge which had been honed to incredible sharpness. Whoosh! The axe descended and when it was again raised, its edge was wet, crimson, dripping, the shininess covered in gore. Again and again it rose and descended. Now both hair and flesh clung to the axe's surface; and the white wall which had been backdrop to the scene was splattered with bits of flesh, bone and brain matter.

Click! He touched the pause button and the VCR stopped. He was breathing fast. He had viewed this scene in the movie many times before, rewinding and rerunning it over and over until his pulse raced and he was always compelled to stop the recorder at this point and wait until his pulse slowed and he could catch his breath. Then he advanced the scene and now he could see what the axe had been striking. Bodies, or parts of bodies, lay scattered everywhere. In the foreground lay a hand, palm up as though in supplication. In the background, propped against the blood-splattered wall, was a head, eyes wide, and mouth open in the beginning or end of a scream. Once again he stopped the tape. He smiled grimly to himself. He had viewed many movies with these scenes and others like them for years now, never quite understanding their fascination, but reveling in the feelings they gave him and the emotions they aroused. That pleasure had been all and enough. Now, however, he knew why he so delighted in such films, the reason he was compelled to view them over and over. Some would call the scenes gruesome, sickening, awful, but he knew them now for what they really were. They were the pattern, the instructions sent to him so that he could learn. By viewing these movies he had learned the way, the method for the end. He was now ready to give them fitting punishment. He would give justice to those who had so wantonly changed his life all those years ago.

FRIDAY

It was early morning in Bannah, North Dakota, and the sounds of the school bell echoed in the Bannah High School corridors, as members of the senior class, individually or in groups of two or three, streamed into the home room classroom. Penny Strickland, seventeen-year-old daughter of Sheriff Glenn *Red* Strickland, had dropped slightly behind the rest of her classmates because of her right leg being in a cast. The cast was rubbing and itching something terrible. She was glad this was the last class before lunch. Maybe then she could stuff a handkerchief in the top as padding or something, or poke in a pencil and scratch! She slid into her desk and positioned her crutch carefully beside her seat, so as not to cause any obstruction of the aisle between the desk rows. The class room was bright and cheerful with large windows that allowed maximum lighting. This was the new section of the school which had been added only two years ago to accommodate the growing number of people who had infiltrated the small community these past two years.

Penny looked around at all the new faces in her class, as well as the familiar faces she had known forever, or at least all her school years. If it had not been for the influx of new people, there would only have been twenty students graduating this year, the same twenty students, for the most part, who had begun school together with her in kindergarten and had shared all the joys and traumas of their young lives. But now the class had at least doubled in size and she was just beginning to be familiar with the names and personalities of the newcomers.

"How long will you be in your cast, Penny?" Lynn Christman, her English teacher asked, turning from the green chalk board where she had been writing a long list of book titles and their authors.

"If all goes well, I should get my walking cast and be rid of these darned crutches next week, at least that is what Dr. Hardin says," Penny answered.

Sandy Reed in the row of desks beside Penny's, leaned over the aisle and whispered, "What about the hay ride?"

Penny frowned and concentrated on getting her Literature book from her bag. "Don't ask," was all she whispered back before the class started. This was the last day before the winter break. Christmas would be a week from tomorrow and at 3:30 p.m., they would be out of school for more than two glorious weeks.

"I've written another story, Miss Christman," Betsy Klein said, approaching the teacher's desk and holding out a sheaf of papers. Penny and Sandy exchanged glances. Betsy was a chubby girl who wore thick glasses and, it seemed, had had a perpetual case of acne since sixth grade. She was not very popular among her fellow students; and, for that matter, was not a particularly bright student. She did fancy herself a writer of mysteries though and had a following of some of the other less popular students with whom she shared her latest literary efforts. She also gave them to Miss Christman; who, if not a fan, at least accepted them graciously. It was part of the job for a small town English teacher.

"Thank you, Betsy," Miss Christman said, taking the papers and placing them under a paperweight at the corner of her desk. "I'll try and read it before the day's end."

Miss Christman went back to the board where she had written her list of books. There was a buzz of barely contained whispers and an increased amount of paper shuffling and rattling. "I know this is the last day of school before the break," Miss Christman gently chided, "but right now you may all begin copying down this list of books. You may select any one of these you wish to read over the holidays. I will expect a book report on my desk when you return to school. Also," she said, as she wrote the words on the blackboard as she spoke them, "this book report will account for one third of this semester's English grade."

There was a loud groan from the class.

"Oh, may we do more than one if we like?" Betsy Klein asked enthusiastically.

"I wonder why no one has ever bothered to stuff her in a dumpster or something," Sandy mouthed to Penny.

"You may do as many as you like, Betsy," Miss Christman smiled.

Jim Easter poked Penny from his seat behind her. Penny half turned and snatched the note Jim was practically pushing under her arm.

"*Betsy's nose should be full of it after all her brown nosing,*" Jim had written in his bold handwriting. Penny grinned and tried to conceal the note in her text book.

"Penny," Miss Christman said, approaching the desk with her hand held out. "Would you like to share the message with the rest of the class?"

Penny's face blanched and then turned a clashing red to the pink sweater she was wearing; she met Miss Christman's eyes and registered a mute appeal.

Lynn Christman took the note, read it, and then crumpled it in her hand as she walked back to sit at her own desk at the front of the class. "We won't share this one with the class," she answered the appeal, "but both you and James may each select three of the books on the board instead of just one, and I won't accept any excuses for the reports not being on my desk on the morning you return to school."

Penny, red faced, felt angry and ashamed at the same time. She would have plenty to say to Jim at lunch. When the class bell finally rang, Penny waited for the rest of the students to make their hasty exit before she, with clumsy cast and crutches, started her slow way out. As she neared the door, Miss Christman stopped her. "Penny, I would have expected better from you."

Penny opened her mouth to say she had not been the one to write the note, but bit her lip instead. "I'm sorry," she murmured and hurried as best she could from the room before Miss Christman could think of any further punishment to inflict on her. She liked Miss Christman best of any of the teachers she had. The English teacher had been one of the several new instructors needed to handle the overflowing class rooms and seemed to understand the students better than some of the older teachers did. Penny hated it when she was called down for something, especially in Miss Christman's class. As she made her way to the cafeteria, she began to feel angrier with Betsy than Jim. It was, after all, really all her fault this day was going so badly.

Penny found her usual group already assembled at the big table in the corner. She made a face at Jim Easter when he offered to get her tray for her. "It's the least you can do for me," Penny said, frowning. "After all, it's all your fault that I got called down in class."

When Jim returned he had an extra carton of chocolate milk on her tray. "They say lots of calcium heals bones faster," he explained at her raised eyebrows. He looked so contrite that Penny giggled, sweeping her long red-blond hair back over her shoulders with her free hand.

"It's impossible to stay mad at you for long," she admitted, placing a straw in the milk carton she had just opened.

"What are you bitching about?" Jim asked in mock anger. "I have to do just as many reports as you do."

"Serves you right for writing notes," Brad Richards commented from across the table. "What'd you say to get Christman upset anyway?"

Penny and Jim both burst into laughter. "Betsy's brown nose," Jim said. All eyes at the table turned to look at Betsy Klein who sat alone at a small table by the door. Feeling their look, she glared back at them, then returned her attention to the book she was reading.

"If Christman wasn't making us do these stupid reports," Jim Easter said, "we'd know all our semester grades before vacation was over. They'll all be posted Monday."

Tracy Wilkins laid down her fork and wiped her mouth with a paper napkin. "I'll stop by the school Monday afternoon," she said, "and then I'll call all you guys with our grades."

"That's great!" Penny said, smiling at her friend. "Wait until I get home from the doctor's office then come over for awhile. I'll be needing some good company by then with this boring weekend ahead of me."

"You were going to tell me about the hay ride," Sandy Reed reminded Penny as she slid onto the chair next to her friend, and began to open her own carton of milk.

"There's nothing to tell," Penny groaned. "Daddy and I had a big fight about it last night and the final word is I can't go!" She almost spat the last remark.

"Didn't you tell him," Jim asked from across the table, "that we would be sure to take care of your cast? We can find a place for you to sit where you can keep the leg stretched out and all."

"I told him! I used every argument and excuse I could think of, even invented some new ones but it was no use. He still said '*No!*' in that tone of his that means it's final!"

"I suppose that means Billy won't be going either," Tracy now chimed in, as she took a bite of the French fries from her plate and chewed.

"Billy's little brother has the measles, didn't you know?" Penny said. "The whole family's kind of quarantined, at least through the weekend. Billy's mom won't even let him come over to the house. I've never had the measles."

"That's a hell of a note to come home from college for," Jim laughed.

"Don't swear," Sandy grinned at him, "especially with your mouth full. It's not good manners."

"I'll teach you girls about manners tonight," Jim shot back.

"Maybe it's a good thing I'm not going," Penny laughed, opening her second carton of milk. "I'd really be odd woman out, without Billy there."

"If you want to talk about *odd*, I suppose you could ask Betsy Klein to go along, if there aren't enough people," suggested Ted Campbell. He stood up and picked up his tray to carry it to the window where other students were depositing the remains of their lunch.

James Easter made an obscene gesture at Ted's back and continued his conversation. "Really, Pen, it isn't going to be nearly as much fun without you and Billy."

"You could postpone the hay ride until Penny is out of her cast," Brad Richards suggested. They all knew that he was really teasing.

"I guess I could . . ." Jim began in a thoughtful voice.

"Oh no, Jim," Penny protested. "We've all been planning this hay ride for weeks. You can always have another one when I get out of the cast."

"That's it!" Jim Easter smiled at her, "a 'Penny Strickland Freedom Hay Ride!'"

"We'll decorate the wagon in red, white and blue streamers and put a big sign on the side, *Penny's Freedom Ride*," Marcia Nye chimed in.

Penny rolled her eyes at her friend. "You guys are just too much," she laughed. "It'll be my best Christmas present, even if it does come after Christmas!" Penny wondered at her own generosity. She had really been looking forward to the first hay ride of the season. Then two weeks earlier she had suffered a spiral fracture of her right leg during cheer leading practice when the last of a series of cartwheels had gone wrong. *Oh well,* she thought, *this is my first gesture of it being better to give than to receive for this Christmas season.* Later she was to remember that she might have been able to prevent the hay ride by asking them to postpone it but at that time, she had not wanted to spoil anyone else's fun.

"Here, load your things on my tray," Paula Whitedeer said, seeing Penny attempt to manipulate both her lunch tray and her crutches. Paula was the seventeen-year-old sister of Charles Whitedeer who was deputy to Penny's father in the now nine-man Bannah sheriff's department.

"I think I can manage," Penny began.

"I'll take both your trays." It was a deep voice and the two girls turned in surprise to see William Hein, their history teacher, who had come up behind them. He was a tall, slender man in his mid thirties with merry blue eyes and chestnut hair just beginning to show a bit of silver at the edges.

"Oh no, Mr. Hein," Paula protested. "That's not really necessary."

"Sure it is," Hein said and picked up the trays before the girls could protest further. "You have just about enough time to get your books from your locker and get to my class on time if you don't have to juggle those trays. I'm allowed to be late for class, but you aren't!"

The two girls smiled their thanks at the favor and started for the stairs. "Isn't he a hunk?" Paula stage whispered as they neared their lockers.

Penny giggled. "Too bad it isn't girls he's interested in."

"What do you mean?"

"Don't tell me you haven't heard the rumors about him and Mr. Jacobs?"

"You really don't believe all that, do you?" Paula asked, color suffusing her dark skin.

"You haven't seen him in anyone else's company, have you?" Before Paula could answer, Penny smiled. "I rest my case."

Paula changed the subject as the girls dug their history books from their lockers. "I'm going to the library tomorrow morning. Would you like me to see if I can find the books you need to do your reports on?"

"Thanks loads," Penny smiled, "but I have study hall second period this afternoon and I thought I'd see what I could find in the school library. But if you tell me what you picked, I'll see if I can find it for you."

"I thought I'd finally read *To Kill a Mockingbird,*" Paula said. "Miss Christman sure picked some out-of-date books, didn't she?"

"Part of the college list, I think. Actually it is not so bad, I've got that one at home and have read it two or three times. It belonged to my mom," she added wistfully. "Come on over tomorrow and I'll give it to you, or would you just rather have a summary?"

"Nope," Paula smiled her thanks as the two girls entered the history class room, "guess I better read it myself, might leave Christman's favorite part out otherwise!"

"What kept you two?" Mr. Hein asked, turning from the blackboard. "You almost missed the pop quiz." At the look on the two girls' faces he grinned. "Just kidding. Take your seats. I'll try to make this class as painless as possible on the last day."

By 2:15 that afternoon, Penny's leg was still itching madly. She was trying to concentrate on Mr. Tuttle's diagram of the long bones of the human skeleton on the blackboard, but she could scarcely think. She longed for a coat hanger or anything else with which she could relieve the itching.

Mr. Tuttle picked up a piece of green chalk and made several large "X's" across the long bone of the skeleton's right leg. "This is why Miss Strickland is squirming and causing such a disturbance," he said, turning to the class. "This, you will note, is the tibia, the bone Miss Strickland had the misfortune to fracture. Class will soon be over and you can scratch to your heart's content, Penny, meanwhile . . ." He paused and turned back to the diagram, his meaning obvious to Penny and the rest of the students.

Penny pursed her lips and clenched her fists in her lap. *This man is not only a turtle,* she thought miserably, *but a 'turd' as well!* Had Mr. Tuttle's comment come from any of the other teachers, Penny, as well as the rest of her classmates would have burst into laughter. As it was, however, the class sat silent, feeling the remark had been made to hurt rather than to tease.

Sam Tuttle had been principal of Bannah High School as long as Penny could remember. For years the students had called him Mr. Turtle, behind his back, of course, because of his name and a way he had of pulling his neck into his collar in much the same way a turtle would pull its head into its shell.

"He sure spoils the last day of school, doesn't he?" Tracy Wilkins murmured to Penny as they left the class room and made their way down the hallway back to their lockers. "Can I give you a lift home?"

"Thanks, Tracy," Penny replied, tossing her books, except for a couple, into the bottom of the locker then slamming the door and giving the combination lock a quick twist. "I have to drop by the library for the book report books and then I will be ready. I forgot to do it at study hall when I thought I would."

After the short stop at the library, the two girls made their way to the stairs leading down. Tracy carried both sets of books while Penny held crutches in one hand and banister in the other and hopped down each step to the bottom and then, returning one of the crutches to her other hand, walked slowly through the door Tracy held open for her and out into the cold December afternoon. The sun was already low in the western sky and the ugly, square, old, red-brick school building cast a shadow over almost the entire parking area. A brisk, cold wind was blowing, swirling the fine snow that had fallen through the previous night.

"What are you going to do over the holidays?" Penny asked as she eased herself into Tracy's little car.

"Some pretty good ballet company is doing *The Nutcracker* in Bismarck," Tracy said. "Gram got tickets for it and we are going. Other than that, just the usual stuff, I guess. What about you?"

Penny rolled her eyes. "Not a lot with this stupid leg," Penny said. "Dad's so afraid something will happen to me I'll be lucky if I get out of the house."

"He lets you come to school."

Penny stuck out her tongue at her friend. "Haven't you heard, school happens whether you are dying or have a broken neck. It's only fun that never happens if you have so much as the sniffles."

Tracy laughed as she pulled her car out of the school parking lot and down the street toward the Strickland's house. "My Gram's a lot the same," she admitted. "I don't know what our families are going to do when we all go off to college next year." Tracy liked Penny probably more than any of the other kids in her class. "Have you decided where you're going to go to school?" she now asked, guiding the car skillfully up the Strickland's steep driveway.

"I'm going to start at Jamestown Teacher's College," Penny said. "Want to come in for awhile?"

Tracy looked sad as she shook her head. "I guess not," she said. "I better go home and see if there's anything I can do to help Gram before the . . ."

Penny reached over and squeezed her friend's hand. "You don't have to walk on eggs," she laughed. "I'll see you soon and you can tell me all about it."

II

At exactly 3:00 p. m., Sarah Cooley had put the finishing touches on a broccoli and cheese casserole and slipped it into the Strickland's oven. She had been keeping house for Red and his daughter for nearly thirteen years now, ever since Sally Strickland had succumbed to cancer when Penny was only five years old. Although she did not live in the house, she still managed the Stricklands and their affairs more like a second mother and grandmother than merely a housekeeper. She had even offered to come in on weekends after Penny had broken her leg, but had been assured that the two Stricklands could manage what absolutely needed to be done. Now she sighed and slipped into her coat ready to leave. Pulling on her snow boots she found herself breathing heavily. She knew she had put on extra pounds over the last few years but now shook her gray head in wonderment. "Christmas is not the time to be thinking of a diet," she grumbled to the cat as he came to see her off, "but I'm getting as fat as you are, Boots." The gray and white cat rubbed against her legs and purred. She hoped it wasn't in agreement. Her own husband, Carl, would be home from the mine at 6:00, and she wanted to make sure that he, too, had a good hot supper waiting for him. "Maybe I'll just *bake* that chicken tonight," she said to the cat, stroking his plump underside and moving to the door. She had left a note as to when the casserole would be done and they could manage from there.

As she left the house, she thought of the up-coming hay ride. Poor little Penny had been so looking forward to going. There had been no need to ask if she was going to be allowed to. From the stormy looks that passed between father and daughter at breakfast, the answer to that one was plain enough. She wondered even now if she shouldn't call the sheriff's office and intercede for Penny. She couldn't see where the hay ride would be such a problem. She sighed and shook her head. *No*, she thought, *it's better not to interfere. He knows how he wants to raise his daughter and it probably wouldn't do for him to back down now.* She smiled, knowing Red Strickland, she also knew the odds of his backing down after making a decision were practically nil. They were both stubborn, father and daughter, she mused while getting into her car, neither willing to give an inch.

III

Brad Richards walked briskly from school to Main Street and his father's hardware store where he generally helped after school and on weekends. This was an especially busy time with people shopping for Christmas presents and his father appreciated the extra hands Brad brought to the store. Brad paused in the doorway of the hardware store and looked up. The strings of green and red Christmas lights that had been strung across the street were already on. Carols came over loudspeakers from Brown's Music Store across the street, filling the entire block with a pleasant sound that he liked. Brad nodded and waved to Mr. Brown who was out sweeping snow from his section of sidewalk in front of the store. *This is a good time to be alive,* Brad thought as he entered the store. School was out and besides the hay ride, there was Christmas to look forward to. He had bought a promise ring for Sandy and he toyed with the idea of giving it to her tonight after the hay ride. He'd just have to see.

"How was school?" his father asked as Brad put on the long work apron he wore to protect his clothes. He was running late and there had not been time to go home and change as he usually did.

"Not bad," Brad said. "We got an English assignment for over the holiday, a book report but that won't be a problem. What would you like me to do?"

"Go to the back storeroom and get some more of those wrench and screwdriver sets. This shelf is nearly empty, they have been selling so well. Then, if you have time, go to the store and pick up the groceries your mother wants for supper. Here's the list." Mr. Richards, a slightly older duplicate of his son, handed Brad a piece of paper as well as the car keys.

"Won't you need me to stay late, Dad?"

Mr. Richards smiled. "Nope, I have everything else pretty much in hand. I thought you'd like to get your supper early so you can get ready and get Sandy early for that hay ride."

Brad smiled his thanks and hurried to the store's back room.

IV

Sandy Reed, too, had hurried to work. Like Brad, she worked in a family business, helping her father in the Piggly Wiggly supermarket he ran. She waved to her father as she hurried to the back of the store where she changed the blouse she had worn to school for the smock hanging there. Sometimes it was not only necessary that she check out the customers, but also that she help carry their purchases to their cars. It helped to have something attractive, which the smock was with the store emblem and her name embroidered over the breast pocket, and yet more washable than some of her pretty school things.

Sandy was a red-haired, hazel-eyed beauty who the previous year had been elected queen of the junior prom. Now as she busily checked out customers, she wondered if she would be able to persuade her parents to allow her to enter the state beauty contest in the spring. She knew that clothes and accessories for such things would cost quite a bit, but she had been saving her pay from her work in the store as well as the evening baby sitting she was able to do after school when her father didn't need her.

"Hi, Sandy!" Brad Richards said as he wheeled his filled shopping cart to her counter.

"My, how domestic," Sandy teased as she began to read the prices off the cans and other items that Brad placed on the conveyer belt in front of her and enter them into her cash register.

Brad placed a six pack of sodas, the last item in his cart, on the belt and leaned across the counter and whispered, "I'll be domestic with you anytime."

Sandy blushed to the roots of her hair. "Dummy! Tell me that this evening, on the hay ride, not here with all this mess!" she said smiling as she placed the sacks of groceries back into the cart.

"I suppose you'll make me carry these to the car myself," Brad laughed.

"I thought you walked over here, like always."

"I've got Dad's car. Mom said she'd pick him up when he closed the store."

The two sweethearts exchanged a meaningful glance as Brad left the store, pushing the cart before him. In less than three hours they would be cuddled up in Jim Easter's wagon, snuggled down in the hay and each other's arms!

A few miles north of Bannah on State Route 23 was the farm where Ted Campbell lived with his family. It was far enough away from the town that he rode the bus from school. Now he hurried up the short dirt road leading from the highway to his home so that he would be sure to have his chores done and his supper out of the way before Jim came by for him on the wagon. He was going to help load some hay from their supply as Jim had said there was not quite enough to fill the wagon at his barn. Then they would go on in to town to pick up the rest of the gang.

Banging through the back door into the hallway where he hung his coat, he found his mother and two little sisters in the kitchen, baking cookies. "Help yourself, why don't you?" his mother laughed as he grabbed a huge handful of cookies from the cooling rack.

"Don't mind if I do, Mom," Ted answered, pounding his way on up the stairs to his room.

"Don't forget to change your clothes before you go out into the barn."

"Why can't I go on the hay ride too?" Ted's little sister Jenny, who was eight years old, asked, following him up the stairs and into his room where she bounced down on his bed.

"Because you're way too little," Ted said over his shoulder, his attention in his closet where he was selecting some coveralls to wear to the barn.

"I'm nearly grown!" Jenny said, pouting.

Ted turned around and sat down on the chair beside his bed, pulling the little girl onto his knee and giving her a hug. "There's lots of times for hay rides for you in the future, Sis," he said, pulling her braids affectionately. "Besides, you'd cramp my style." He stood up, dumped her, giggling, back on to the bed and began to pull on the coveralls.

"Jenny! Come help frost these cookies and don't bug your brother," Ted's mother admonished, her voice drifting up the stairs.

"Ted's going on a hay ride! Ted's going on a hay ride!" Charlotte, his five-year-old sister chanted, jumping up and down.

Ted raced back down the stairs and swung her up in his arms. "You're making the light fixtures shake," he laughed.

"To say nothing of all the dishes in the cupboard," his mother added.

"Ted's got a girlfriend!" Charlotte changed her chant as she wriggled free from his embrace.

Ted pulled her curls and hurried outside, munching one of the cookies he had grabbed earlier. He liked the farm; even some of the more disagreeable farm chores didn't bother him. He was looking forward to attending agricultural college in the fall. He wanted to join his parents in the running of the farm when his education was complete.

As he freshened the straw in the cow barn and got ready to milk, he was thinking of Tracy Wilkins. He hoped some day she would share this farm life with him. Tracy was a quiet, rather plain girl, who loved animals and children. She had dreams of becoming a veterinarian when she got out of school. Well, Bannah wasn't so small that it couldn't support a good veterinarian. Ted smiled to himself thinking of little Tracy trying to pull a calf from an unwilling cow. He looked forward to their evening together. Maybe he'd ask her tonight if she'd wear his class ring.

VI

Marcia Nye hurried home to begin supper. Marcia's father had been killed in a mining accident when she was very small. Her mother had gone to work in the mine office when Marcia had started school. They lived a quiet but comfortable life. An easy-going girl, she had never given her mother any of the problems familiar to parents of most teenagers. She helped around the house without being asked. She tended to her studies and got good enough grades. She dreamed of marrying Jim Easter some day. She knew that both her mother and his parents disapproved of steady dating at their age, but still, her mom admitted Jim was a good, steady boy and certainly would be a "good catch for some girl some day," as she expressed it. Marcia did not like the expression but privately agreed with her mother's opinion of Jim.

Marcia had supper finished and on the table when her mother arrived a little after five p.m.

"Thank you, Dear," her mother said, getting out of her coat and gloves. "I appreciate coming home to a nice, hot meal!"

"Is it getting any colder out?" Marcia asked, setting a steaming mug of herb tea in front of her mother.

"No, I think it's going to be a beautiful night. The moon and stars are all out and it looks so pretty. The weather report said that there was no more snow expected until tomorrow night so you should have a fine night for the hay ride."

The two sat down to a meal of bacon, eggs, hash browned potatoes and toast. "You get ready now, Dear," Marcia's mother said, pushing her plate back after they were finished. "I'll get the dishes for you tonight."

"I've got plenty of time, Mom," Marcia objected, beginning to clear the table.

"Then I'll wash and you dry." Kathryn Nye said, tying an apron around herself. "We'll be done in half the time. Then I'm going to take a long, hot bath with lots of bubbles, and finish that Danielle Steel book I've been reading while you are on that hay ride."

VII

Jim Easter had left school and gone to his father's farm also located north of Bannah. Like Ted Campbell, he liked farming. His father wanted very much for him to come back and work on the farm with him, but his mother hoped he would change his mind and go into either law or medicine. Jim wondered as he fed the cows and brushed the two old farm horses, why everyone's mother thought law or medicine were the only careers worthy of their only sons. His parents had married late in life and Jim was their only child. Now with his father nearing the age where taking it easy would be nice, Jim simply wanted to get agricultural college out of the way and return to Bannah and Marcia Nye. He knew there would be a lot of persuading to be done before his mother would agree to allow him to attend agricultural college. Oh well, there was still half a year before he would have to worry about that.

VIII

Tracy Wilkins drove the six blocks home after dropping Penny Strickland off at her house. Both Tracy's parents had been killed in a boating accident when she was only three years old. They had lived in a suburb of Detroit, and Tracy still had a hazy recollection of her life there and of the grandmother, a stranger to her at that time, who had come to the big, sad house, and quietly soothed away the hurt and fears. As her only remaining relative, her father's mother had taken her back to live with her in Bannah. The house in which they lived was small but comfortable. Tracy's grandmother was not really an old woman, but life for her had been difficult. Her own husband had died at age thirty-six of a sudden heart attack. And after the death of her only son, in the accident, she had, for a time, given up her zest for life. But her responsibility for Tracy had changed that feeling finally. Now with Tracy nearly out of high school, Mrs. Wilkins was rather looking forward to more time alone again. She had many outside interests, and planned to do some traveling when Tracy went to college in the fall.

Tracy walked into the clean, warm kitchen and saw a note propped up on the sugar bowl which sat in the center of the table. *Gone for bridge. Casserole warm in the oven. Have a lovely time this evening. Love, Gram.*

Tracy hurried to her room and changed into the jeans and sweat shirt she would wear on the hay ride. She laid out the down-filled jacket her grandmother had given her as an early Christmas present, saying, "If you are going to sit in that wagon with that young Campbell boy you will need more than his arm to keep you warm." Tracy smiled and hurried back into the kitchen where she ate her dinner and then quickly washed the dishes and put them away. On the bottom of her grandmother's note, she wrote in her neat hand, *Don't wait up for me, I'll tell you all about it in the morning. Love, Tracy.*

SATURDAY

Will Lester was a little drunk, as a matter of fact, he was very drunk. It was nearly 2:00 a. m. on this cold Saturday morning. A considerable amount of snow had fallen in the previous few days. Now the moon shone on a fairy land. Snow and ice crystals shrouded tree branches in grotesque but beautiful figures and shapes. The reflection of the moonlight and the shadows it cast on this expanse of whiteness made the entire area seem mysterious and entrancing, but Will had little inclination to admire the view. He had worked on the Easter farm for the past two years and he felt more like one of the family than an employee. That had made the near blow-up that had occurred between him and Mr. Easter Friday morning even more unpleasant. He regretted the incident, but it had not been fair. Young Jim could think of nothing but that stupid hay ride. He, Will, had wanted to accompany his girl friend on her Christmas vacation, home to meet her family. A couple weeks wouldn't really matter at this time of year, but Mr. Easter had been adamant. No one other than he and Mrs. Easter knew that Will was on parole. One of the stipulations of his being allowed to work on the farm had been that he not leave the area and especially not go out of state without the express consent of his parole officer, and that request had been flatly denied. Will had wanted at least then to take his girlfriend, Mavis, to Bismarck to catch her plane for St. Paul.

Mavis worked as a cook at the Bannah High cafeteria, and they would be separated for almost two weeks. Why couldn't the Easters see there was nothing wrong with that? True, Mavis didn't know he was on parole. Had she known that he had been convicted of rape and assault, he was sure she would not have gone with him.

So he had stormed away from the farm in Mr. Easter's own Ford Bronco and had driven Mavis to Bismarck, stayed with her until her plane had gone, and then he had driven back to Bannah. It was, after all, only about a two-hour trip one way.

Except the two hours back had now become six as, needing what his grandmother had called "Dutch courage" to face the Easters on his return, Will had stopped at the Mirror Bar for a few drinks and a bottle for the rest of the way home. There would be hell to pay in the morning, he was sure. Here it was almost 2:00 and he was driving slowly and carefully, as drunks do, along the last few miles leading back to the farm. The road was not much traveled and had not been plowed since the last snow. In his condition, he was sure glad for four-wheel drive.

He tilted up the bottle for the last swallow and pulled into the road leading to the farm house. As he drove near the barn, he was surprised to see the hay wagon with the team of horses still hitched, standing patiently by the barn door. *That's not right,* he thought, *not at all like young Jim! Jim was very level headed and responsible. He would not have gone to bed, no matter how many nips he and the gang might have shared on the hay ride, without caring for the horses first.*

Will sat in the Bronco for a few minutes, wondering what to do. At last he got out carefully, staggered a bit, then opened the wide barn door and led the horses and wagon into the huge barn. He turned on the overhead lights, illuminating the large room rather dimly at this time of morning, unhitched the still hot and sweaty horses and put them in their respective stalls, debating with himself whether to give them feed or just pitch in a little hay until morning.

"What the hell," he muttered, "no sense wasting the hay on the wagon. I'll just give you fellows a few forks full and young Jim can tend to you tomorrow. I'm sure Big Jim will have plenty to say when he finds out about this."

In the dim light Will did not notice the dark stains covering the hay and the boards of the wagon. It was not until he stepped up on the wagon bed and lifted the first forkful of hay that he noticed something wrong. And then, as he stared at what was caught on the long, sharp tines of the pitchfork, he felt the bile rise up in his throat, and he turned aside, emptying his stomach of several dollars worth of good liquor. Suddenly he wasn't drunk any more.

II

Glen *Red* Strickland, sheriff of Bannah, North Dakota, was deep in a dream. He had just shouldered his rifle and sighted on a beautiful buck deer. As his finger slowly squeezed the trigger, the rifle responded with a large ring. *Ring? That isn't right,* he thought with the logic some people have in their dreams, *a 30-06 makes a bang, a rather loud bang, not a ring!* As the ring repeated, he awoke and realized it was the telephone bell.

He peered at the clock on the night stand beside his bed. In the dim light the luminous dial showed nearly 2:30. *This better be important,* he thought as he reached for the phone. Not yet fully awake, he almost knocked the phone from the stand before wrapping his big hand around the receiver.

"Hello," he growled, "what's the trouble?" In the next instant his feet were on the floor and he was wide awake, forgetting the dream buck and everything else that might have been pleasant that evening. He quickly pulled on his pants and shirt, grabbed mismatched socks which he tangled in his haste to thrust on his feet. Then he stamped into his boots, grabbed the gun belt that hung behind the bedroom door and hurried to the hall for overcoat and cap.

Before leaving the house, he tiptoed quietly to the door of his daughter's room and looked in. Penny lay on her back, her cast leg propped up on pillows. Her hair fell about her face like a cloud. She had one fist under her chin, the way she used to sleep, he remembered, when she was only a tiny baby. He closed her door softly and let himself out. She was used to his callouts at night and seldom awoke anymore. She would not worry if he weren't there when morning came. Besides he usually had the dispatcher call her if he was going to be delayed.

As he got into his car, he turned on the red lights--no siren this close to the house and no traffic at this hour to warn--and began the ten mile trip to the Easter farm. He was remembering the almost violent scene he had with Penny the previous morning. He had been adamant about her not going on the hay ride which had been the highlight of the beginning of the round of parties that would be going on through the Christmas holidays. On and on they had raged at one another until it ended in her hurling accusations of his not loving her, and his returning the fact that for an honor student she was not very bright. "Catch your death," he now mused as he drove along the road. He wondered just what he would find when he got to the Easter farm. James Easter had been somewhat incoherent to say the least. Surely he had misunderstood what the man had said, surely!

Strickland, at age fifty-five, was a widower, and Penny was his only child. He was tall and weighed close to two hundred pounds but the weight was all solid muscle. His once fiery red hair was now flecked with gray and his normally gentle blue eyes glinted with anger at what the person on the telephone had told him.

He had married Sally Miller when he was twenty-eight years old and still unsure of what he wanted for his future. He had attempted to run his father's farm after his death, but it took him only a short time to determine farming was not for him. He had entered college late, and there had met Sally who was finishing her education, looking forward to becoming an art instructor. The two of them had settled down in Bannah, county seat of Murray county, and when Red had decided to run for the position of sheriff, Sally had backed him all the way.

Those first few years had been trying times. He had only been sheriff for two years when the coal mine became embroiled in the worst strike the town had seen in many years. Red was reminded of the passage in the Bible that talked of brother turning against brother and fathers and mothers against their children. The town had been split with some favoring the strikers and their demands while others sided with the "scabs" who eagerly took their places. Where the whole thing would have ended was now anyone's guess. Things had culminated, however, in the fire which had taken the lives of Ben Owens, the mine supervisor, and his wife, Marjorie, and had severely burned Donna and Donald, the Owens' fourteen-year-old twins. The children had been flown to a burn center in Minneapolis; and Red, who had not thought of that night in many years, found himself wondering what had ever become of them. At that time he had been forced to deal with an angry and bitter town and the welfare of the Owens children had not seemed of any importance. He wondered now with his maturity and added years of experience if he should have followed up on them and helped in some way to salve not only the physical pain but the emotional pain that must have resulted from such devastating trauma. Now it seemed his town would once more be thrown into a horror too bizarre to comprehend.

He remembered that he and Sally had been as happily married as most couples they knew. It had been nearly ten years, however, before their daughter, Penelope, had been born. Sally had left her teaching job and had concentrated her efforts, full time, at being a wife and mother.

Then, sadly, they had learned that Sally had liver cancer only five years after their daughter had been born. In a surprisingly short time, four months to be exact, after finding out this devastating news, Sally had died, leaving Red with a full-time job, and a five-year-old daughter to raise.

Arriving finally, Red stopped his musing and began the turn into the road leading to the Easter farm.

III

He was shivering. Whether this was from the cold or from the ecstasy of what he had done, he could not be sure. It had all been so easy. He had given them hot chocolate and commended their caroling efforts. He knew they had been drinking liquor along the way which would just speed up the effects of the Trazodone he'd used to sedate them. Then he had been more than clever, he had put on a long, oversized plastic raincoat as well as throw-away plastic gloves. Then he had placed a pair of over-sized woolen socks over his snow boots. Just let them try to identify any boot prints! He had then padded across the carpet, out into the cold, starry night and backed his car out of the unattached garage. He had then just followed their hay wagon, at a discrete distance of course, until the driver became sleepy and unable to continue the journey. He felt himself more than clever.

Now he finished undressing, adding pants, shirt, T-shirt, shorts, and both pair of socks to the heavy duty garbage bag, leaving out only the boots. Then he hid the bag and boots far back in the walk-in closet in his bedroom and lay on his bed, remembering what it had been like. His rage had surprised him. He had not realized how much he hated them all, boys and girls alike, the beautiful, smart, normal kids!

Most of them had been fast asleep. The girl, what was her name, oh yes, Sandy, had drunk less of the chocolate than had the others. It had been necessary to tie her. Then he bathed her face in snow, stimulating her waking. She had stared, uncomprehending, unbelieving. She had recognized him! He had made her watch the mutilation of her friends. He had even promised her that if she was still he might let her live. Of course, he knew that was not possible; and, he was sure, down deep inside, she knew it too.

"I don't understand," she had moaned when her turn to die had come. "Why are you doing this?" So he had told her as he threw the bodies and parts of bodies of her friends back in the hay wagon like so much cord wood. He had explained how it had been necessary for him to return to Bannah, to avenge the great wrong that had been done to him and his family. But she didn't understand. There was only one person in his entire life who had understood him, who had loved him and stood by him no matter what. But then he had stood by her too, hadn't he? Oh yes, he was really avenging both of them; although, perhaps, just perhaps, she would not agree.

"Holy Mary, Mother of God," Sandy had whispered. "Pray for us sinners now and at the hour of our death." She had still been whispering her prayers when he had put the knife to her throat and slit it from ear to ear. He had almost felt sorry for her. He hoped her prayers had gotten her the absolution she had sought. He really had been much kinder to them than anyone had ever been to him. Except for the girl, none of them had really known what was happening to them. He had mercifully killed them before undressing them and continuing with the mutilations. Oh yes, he had to undress them, didn't he? He had to look on those perfect bodies, those perfect faces and then make sure they would never be considered perfect again. His only regret was that the little Strickland bitch hadn't been among them. He would have had special treatment for her. Oh well, perhaps there would be other opportunities. Now he thought of Sandy's eyes: big, dark, full of shock, sorrow, and what else? Those eyes were not unlike the eyes in the movie, his favorite movie! He regretted that he had been so easy on the rest of them.

He lay across his bed and waited for sleep. He had been very careful to do his work in such a remote area that it would be a long while before the wagon and its contents were discovered. Now, if only the weather would co-operate, a heavy snow would obliterate any remaining signs of his presence and return home. Now he would sleep, a deep, dreamless, blameless sleep and in the dark hours just before dawn he would arise, leave his room and go to her.

IV

Five a. m. and five men sat in James Easter's kitchen. This room was warm, spacious, with all the modern conveniences there to attest to the prosperity of at least one North Dakota wheat and cattle farmer. Each man was lost deep in his own contemplations of what he had witnessed in the past few hours. Each tried to come to terms with, to understand what he had seen in the dark dawn on the awful trip each had made with Sheriff Strickland. But no matter how they rethought, reexamined, reviewed the events, each man knew his life in this sleepy little town of Bannah would forever be altered by the events of the past hours.

Red stared down into his coffee cup. He wrapped his hands around it, hoping to gain from its surface some warmth against the coldness that had wrapped itself around his heart. He wondered just how much carnage one could witness before the mind became numbed to what the eyes saw. He felt he had reached and surpassed that point.

Everyone jumped at the jangling of the telephone mounted on the wall next to the refrigerator. Red knew without a doubt what the call was, just not who might be making it. He motioned the others to keep their seats as he rose and moved quickly to answer. "Sheriff Strickland," he barked into the receiver and then paused as he listened to the conversation on the other end.

"Bob," he said, "get Matt and Buddy up and tell them they have an early shift. Tell them to call me here and I'll give them instructions." He paused to listen. "If any others call tell them there has been a problem and they will be getting a visit from us. Get those two deputies in and on the phone to me, ASAP!"

Reaching the Easter farm—a lifetime ago, it seemed now—he had been confronted by an hysterical Molly Easter, a white faced, blank eyed Will Lester; and James Sr. himself, who was gray, shrunken, and who had seemed to age far past his sixty years. Strickland had tried to gain some sense from the confused babble which greeted him. Finally he had made them all sit down while he called Ben Harden, doctor to the Easters as well as the rest of Bannah for the past twenty years.

When the doc arrived, he took one quick look and immediately administered a powerful sedative to Molly and made her lie down in their room where she soon fell into a troubled sleep. Then the four men went out to the barn to join Charles Whitedeer, Strickland's chief deputy, who had arrived minutes before and had preceded them there.

Red had already learned, if somewhat incoherently, that there had apparently been several murders committed in connection with the hay ride held that night. The bodies, dismembered and buried in the hay on the wagon, had been discovered by Lester through the expeditious if grisly method of finding a severed head, unrecognizable at this point, that had been stuck on the tines of the pitchfork with which he had attempted to offer hay from the wagon to the horses he had unhitched and placed in their stalls.

When the sheriff and the doctor had reached the wagon they were shocked to see that the hay had been removed and that the dismembered bodies had been covered with horse blankets.

"Who moved things!" Red roared as he entered the barn and saw what had happened to the evidence before him.

A shame-faced Will looked at him in mute appeal. "I couldn't just leave 'em like that," he said. "They were all . . . bare . . . exposed. Besides, I didn't move anybody, any thing, I just covered them up!"

Red stared at Will Lester until the latter dropped his eyes and hung his head. Red then grasped Will by the shoulders and shook him. "What else did you do?" he demanded, trying to keep his voice level.

Will pointed to a large box standing near the wagon. "Their things," he said. "They were all tossed into the back corner of the wagon, and I . . . I thought their folks might like to have 'em back, without all that blood. I just wiped them off a little and put them in that old box."

Red looked at Dr. Harden and shrugged helplessly. "Didn't move anything, huh? I guess you know," he said, fixing Will Lester with a hostile glare, "you probably destroyed any evidence we might have found."

Will had broken down then and had tried to flee the barn in tears. But he was restrained by one of the other deputies who had arrived and led to a corner of the barn away from the wagon. There the deputy quietly and skillfully began to calm and question him.

Red circled the wagon and examined the bodies, now uncovered by another deputy who was methodically taking pictures with a large camera and flash attachment, old by modern standards but still working. Not one body appeared to remain completely whole. Some of the youngsters appeared to have been bludgeoned to death from what he could see of crushed skulls and broken parts, while others seemed to have been hacked with what must have been an extremely sharp instrument like an axe. Still others had suffered multiple stab wounds to all parts of their bodies. A head that he surprisingly recognized as Sandy Reed's hung at an impossible angle. It had been nearly severed from her body. The head which Will had first speared on the pitchfork apparently was that of Jim Jr. No wonder his mother had been in hysterics. Red fought the bile that rose into his throat. "I'll boil that son-of-a-bitch in oil when I catch him," he muttered to himself, not trying to suppress the sob that escaped him. "If it takes me the rest of my life, I swear I'll get that bastard!"

It was a little after 6:00 a. m. when the State Police lab technicians from Bismarck finally arrived. Bannah, like many small towns, had no facilities for such work and depended upon the state for technical support. The technicians had gathered what information, photos, and samples they could at the scene. "It is not going to be easy," the technician in charge of the crew remarked to Red as they stood to one side watching the activity swirl around them. "No crime scene, everything re-arranged and messed up here. We'll do what we can under the circumstances."

"I'm waiting for a guy with his pack of hounds," Red told Jerry Singer, one of the crime scene investigators. "Hang around and we'll see if we can't find where all this happened. Maybe, just maybe there'll be more things for you to take back to Bismarck with you."

"Trained tracking dogs?" Singer asked.

Strickland shook his head. "No, just a pack of hunting hounds but they have managed to find a couple of missing kids so I'm hoping this will pan out." He continued, "What about the bodies? Dr. Hardin here is the County Coroner as well as our local physician. Any reason why you have to take them all the way to Bismarck?"

The tall, blond-haired man shook his head. "Your morgue facilities are as good as any," he said. "Your doc knows what is needed and has the state medical examiner's number if there are questions. It is your case, do what you have to. We'll keep in touch." After that, all quietly went about their various tasks. The remains of the six students were gathered in body bags and carried to the two hearses of the Wilmington Funeral Home who transported them to the Bannah hospital morgue.

Red returned to the kitchen and asked if he might use the phone. James Easter, still sitting at the kitchen table with a dazed expression on his face, merely nodded. Red dialed his office and when Buddy Schmidt answered, gave him the bare facts of the case with instructions for the deputies to go and speak personally to each family. "I'll be there to see each one of them as soon as I've got everything cleared up here. Oh, and Buddy," he added, "I don't want this discussed with anyone but the kids' families. It's going to be hard enough keeping the rumors down so tell everyone to keep their mouths shut."

After his phone conversation he returned once more to the barn. "I want to talk to that Lester boy a little more," Red said. "I'm still uneasy about the fact that he did all that rearranging before letting anyone know the kids were killed."

"Do you think he did it?" Whitedeer asked.

"Given his previous record . . ." Red trailed off as the two men left the barn and glanced up at the second story window where Will Lester had his quarters. He sniffed the air and wrinkled his nose. "Wonder what he's using for firewood," he said as the two men approached the outside stairway. "Smells a little like old sheep."

Will Lester was reluctant to open the door more than a few inches when he saw who was standing on the landing. "I'll come down," he offered, beginning to close the door. The sheriff stuck the toe of his boot into the crack and gave a mighty push. Will Lester staggered back at the suddenness of the movement and the two men entered.

"What are you burning?" Red demanded, walking purposefully to the Franklin stove that sat in the middle of the living room.

Lester attempted to interpose himself between the sheriff and the stove, but Red pushed him aside and opened the door. He reached in, heedless of the smoldering cloth, and pulled out the remnants of something brown and corduroy.

Will Lester sat down and looked at the two men helplessly. "It's not what you think . . ." he began.

"Go down and get an evidence bag," Red said to Charles as he took a chair opposite Will Lester. "We'll need to do some work on this," he added grimly.

"I knew that's what you'd think," Will began. "That's why I thought it best to . . . to . . ." He got to his feet and paced the room in agitated strides. "I was wearing the jacket when I came home. I . . . I kind of got blood on it when I . . . well, you know . . ."

The sheriff raised both eyebrows. "Will," he said, keeping his voice soft and almost gentle, "I'm almost afraid to ask what else you've done this evening. First you move the bodies, then you re-arrange the evidence in the wagon, *and now you try and burn a jacket because you say you are innocent!"* He had leapt to his feet and shouted the last at the now terrified Lester.

Charles Whitedeer reentered the room, a plastic bag in his hands. He took what remained of a brown corduroy jacket from Red's hands and placed it in the bag which he then sealed and labeled.

"Go on," Red said, turning his attention back to Will Lester, "and, for God sake, sit down!"

Will sank back into his chair and dangled his hands between his knees.

"Why didn't you just give the jacket to us in the first place?" Red demanded.

"I told you . . . I knew you'd think what you're both thinking now. I took the damned jacket off before I went to the house to get Mr. Easter. I didn't want him to see me with all that blood. It was going to be hard enough to . . . to tell him . . . well, you know . . ."

"If you had brought it to me in the barn . . . or at least told me about it when I was talking to you in the barn, you'd be in a hell of a lot less trouble than you are in now. Don't you see, Will, everything you are doing is making it seem more and more like you know more about all this than you're telling us."

Will got up and walked to the window that overlooked the driveway. "I wouldn't of hurt those kids," he said, not looking at the sheriff or his deputy. "I never hurt anyone."

"That's not what your record shows," Red said quietly. "Rape and assault don't sound like someone who wouldn't hurt anyone."

Will came to stand before the sheriff. "It wasn't true," he said.

"Where have I heard that one before?" Charles Whitedeer put in, leaning against the door with one hand resting lightly on the butt of his gun. His stance was plain to read. There was going to be no escape.

"Want to talk about it?" Red Strickland asked quietly.

"About what?"

"Friday night."

Lester shook his head. "There's nothing to talk about," he said miserably. "I want to talk about my arrest and . . . being in prison and all . . ."

"Well?" Red prompted.

"I was going with this girl," Will began, and resumed his agitated pacing. "She came on to me pretty strong, so I invited her up to my room. I was working at a feed store and had a little place above the store. Well, she came up and . . . well . . . we went to bed. After it was all over, her brother comes bustin' into the place, and as soon as she saw him, she hollers rape. I didn't know, until then, I swear to God, I didn't know she was only fifteen."

"Where were you?" Red questioned.

"Still in bed," Will said, dropping his gaze to the floor. "She told her brother I'd forced her and said I'd kill her if she didn't do what I wanted. He came after me, with a knife."

"That's not what your record shows," Red said.

"I was fighting for my life," Will went on. "I managed to kick the knife out of his hand and then I hit him. We went at it pretty good and I guess I hit him harder than I meant to, anyway, when the cops came, the guy was unconscious."

"What about the knife?" Red demanded.

Will flopped back onto the chair. "While the fight was going on, the girl got dressed, hid the knife somewhere, and told the cops the same story she told her brother. She said when her brother had come to rescue her, I'd half-killed him. Without the knife to prove it was self defense, I didn't have a chance!"

Red and Charles exchanged a look. "Then why in hell did you have to pull this stupid thing?" Red thundered, pointing to the evidence bag.

Will looked miserably up at the sheriff. "I figured it would be just like then," he said. "I had a fight with Mr. Easter, the kids died, and here was my coat, covered in blood."

Red Strickland got to his feet and laid a heavy hand on Will's shoulder. "Listen to me!" he said emphasizing every word carefully and slowly. "There is a lot you are leaving unsaid, about the rape and about this. You have a lot more explaining to do."

Red told one of the other deputies to watch Lester and he and Whitedeer left the small apartment and went down stairs.

"Think he's telling the truth?" Whitedeer asked.

"Probably. The story is too stupid to be a lie." The two men went back into the barn and presented the evidence bag to the crime lab boys.

At eight o'clock the group again assembled in the kitchen. Will Lester had been persuaded to join the men and he sat staring at his hands which picked nervously at one another on his lap. Red Strickland cleared his throat and looked at the pale man. "Now that everything has calmed down, let's go over again what you told us earlier. You know about finding the head . . . and what you did then."

"Well, like I told you before, I was dead tired, maybe a little drunk, more than a little mad that young Jim hadn't put away the team. I wanted to get everything over as soon as possible; so, rather than their usual feed, I just grabbed the pitchfork to throw some of the hay from the wagon in to satisfy the team until morning. I figured it would be that much less to unload come daylight. The fork kind of stuck on something and I gave it an extra push and it went in kind of squashy, like a melon. I heaved and up came . . . well, you know . . . the head. I thought first it was some kind of a joke. You know, one of those things you can get in a joke store. Then I saw all that blood and I knew it was no joke. I dropped the fork and kind of threw up outside. Then, I don't know what came over me; I still couldn't believe it was real so I started taking out the hay. I tried to be careful, digging through. Well . . . the first thing that showed up was a pile of clothes just tossed in the back corner of the wagon. I don't know why I did it. I got that box and put them in. It just seemed right." He paused and took a sip from the cup of now cold coffee that rested on the table before him.

"Go on," Red prompted, still wishing he could break Will Lester's neck, or at least bruise him severely.

"Well, I kept digging and found . . . you know . . . parts . . . I got down, found some blankets and . . . covered . . . When I saw all that blood on my jacket, I went and changed into another one before getting Mr. Easter. I'm really not too sure what happened after that until you got here."

"Pretty calm and organized, weren't you?" Charles Whitedeer said, sarcastically. "I would have run like hell if it'd been me. I sure wouldn't have hung around *arranging things.*"

Red Strickland shook his head almost imperceptibly at his deputy. "Just a few more questions, Will," Red said, uncrossing his legs and leaning forward across the table. "Where did you go last night?"

Will Lester turned white. He jumped to his feet. "You don't think, surely you don't think I had anything to do with this!"

"Simmer down, Son," the sheriff said. "I'm not accusing you of anything. I'm just trying to find out if you noticed anything different on your way home. That is before you saw what was here."

Will slowly sat back down. "No," he said, "I was driving awful careful, it being the boss's car and all. I was just surprised when I got here and found the team had not been unhitched. Jim is . . . was . . . a good kid. He loved animals and sure wouldn't neglect them like that. I was a little hot under the collar when I saw those poor horses standing there in the cold. I guess that upset me so much I didn't take time to notice anything else. Like I said, I just wanted to get them fed and then me into bed."

"You still haven't told me where you were," Strickland asked again and his frown was so fierce the younger man quailed before it.

Lester looked from the sheriff to his employer and back again. "I went to Bismarck." He spoke so low that the other men strained to hear him. "I took Mavis to the airport and then came home and stopped at the bar for a few drinks."

James Easter looked at the young man and shook his head. "Even though you were ..." he began.

"Let's not worry about that now," Strickland said. "Can you verify that alibi, Will?"

The farm hand hung his head. "Just call Mavis," he said. "I'll give you her folks' phone number, and, yeah, there were a bunch of guys at the Mirror Bar who saw me and the bartender will tell you I was the last one to leave."

"Would you have any idea," Charles Whitedeer spoke again, "about how long the team might have been standing there before you got home?"

"Well . . ." Will scratched his chin thoughtfully, "I don't think that wagon had been back for long. The horses hadn't really cooled down much. I noticed that when I unhitched them."

Red nodded. "How long do you think they would have remained where they were before they gave up and started for home?"

"Depends," Will said, getting to his feet and pacing up and down the room again. "Probably with the smell of death and blood all around, they would have hightailed for home as soon as they were left standing alone."

"Did they seem nervous or skittish when you got there?" Charles now put in.

Will shook his head, "They were just standing there, patiently waiting to be unhitched."

Shortly after that, the two men excused themselves and went back to the barn. The barn showed evidence of the hurried but thorough examination. Red would like to have handled the entire investigation himself; but Bannah was far too small to maintain the equipment and the men needed for the type of investigation he feared this case would present. In his more than twenty years of being a law enforcement officer in Murray County, he had not seen a case of this magnitude and complexity. As a matter of fact, the only murder he could remember occurred when he was still a comparatively young man. Robinson and Simmons, he never would forget those names, had been two crusty old farmers who had gotten in to an argument over a debt. The end result was that the two men had shot one another. These murders could have been done by outsiders, a group of Satan worshipers—he had heard there were cults like that operating in his area—but somehow he doubted it.

He knew the people, or at least he thought he knew the people of Bannah: he felt this crime had been committed by someone known to at least some of the kids, someone they trusted. He also knew one thing more, no matter how many outside officers came in, how many questions they asked the people, they would still need him, to be sure the answers they were getting were the right ones. He knew how close-mouthed the hard working German-Russian coal miners would be about this. They would form a protective band to insulate and isolate the families and each other from this tragedy. Outsiders would never be able to penetrate that shield. The wheat and cattle farmers who preferred to do their shopping and take their pleasures on Saturday evenings in the town would be the same.

But there were the newcomers. Bannah had gotten a new power plant as well as the first real industry outside of the coal mine to come into this Dakota area. A manufacturer of farm machinery had opened a plant just outside town less than a year ago. Between the building of the power plant and the new factory, there were at least two thousand people he really didn't know that well.

New churches had been built to accommodate the growth of the congregations. For the first time in the town's history, it had become necessary to build an addition to the school, just for the increase in high school students. Prior to that all twelve grades had ample room in the old red brick school house located in the center of town. The teaching staff had been increased dramatically in the past two years.

Red mused now at the number of faces he saw every day to which he still could not put names. His own department had put on additional staff as well as now requiring a twenty-four hour work day. The once insulated community had grown; and, with that growth had come what, madness? If not that, then at least noise, crowding and problems that Bannah had not seen before.

While he stood there, leaning against the door frame and trying to figure out where the investigation should go from here, a red pickup came driving up the lane. Charles was waiting for it at the large circle drive; and he walked out to join him and the driver of the truck.

Bill Jenkins climbed down from the cab of his truck and shook hands with the two law officers. From the back of the vehicle came the whining and barking of several dogs. "Hi, Sheriff, I got here as quickly as I received Chuck's phone call. I brought three of my best dogs."

"Leave the dogs in the truck until we can show you what we've got in mind," Red said as the three men began walking toward the barn.

They entered and Jenkins looked around as his eyes adjusted to the dimmer light. They narrowed as he noted the dark stains on the floor in front of the door. "Blood?" he asked.

Red nodded. "Chuck gave you an idea of what happened over the phone; but I wanted you to see for yourself how the blood seeped down through the hay and the boards of the wagon onto the floor. You see the amount here. There is more inside the barn but not enough to account for the number of bodies we found. There's got to be a lot more blood out where they were killed; and, maybe, just maybe, some of it trailed on the ground from there all the way back here when the horses came in. Think your dogs can pick up the trail, backtrack it to wherever these kids were killed?"

Jenkins produced a pipe from his coat pocket; and, putting it in his mouth, chewed on it thoughtfully as he looked down at the stains. Red had never seen him without it, he had never seen him light it either. Jenkins walked around the stains in a big circle, then he followed them toward the door. "Maybe…we can try. The scent won't be good with all the snow and cold though."

Without another word, he returned to the pickup, opened the cage door; and, as each dog jumped to the ground, snapped a leash to its collar. The dogs strained eagerly at their leashes. Bill took them further inside the barn. "It's warmer back here toward the back," he called over his shoulder. "The scent should be better back here. I don't want to confuse them but I want them to get a smell of the wagon, the horses and the blood." He showed the dogs the stains on the floor, patiently waiting until each dog had a sniff, then he led them out; and again showed them the blood-soaked snow at the edge of the driveway leading to the barn. "Seek!"

The dogs whined eagerly, and as Jenkins unsnapped their leashes, circled, and then, with noses to the ground, began to work their way down the lane. Bill tossed his pickup keys to Charles and told him to wait until they were at the end of the lane near the main road, then to follow them with the truck. The crime scene investigator walked up then, put a few bags and boxes in the back and climbed in the truck beside the deputy. Bill and the sheriff set off behind the dogs at a steady, swift walk.

When they reached the intersection, the dogs seemed to have lost the trail, milling back and forth in obvious puzzlement. "This road has been plowed since last night; and the oil from the cars, the number of travelers would sure throw them off," Jenkins explained. "But, maybe we will find the trail again. It will just take a little more time."

Jenkins took the dogs back to the truck which Whitedeer had parked off the side of the road, opened the back and put two of the dogs inside, leaving only the lead dog now back on its leash, standing beside him. "This will take Ginger and me a little while, and I'd rather you not be with us; I'll call you when she finds the trail again." He and the dog then took off walking along the side of the road a bit between the margin and the deep wheel tracks. The sheriff and the others sat down on the fenders of the truck to watch.

Jenkins and the dog walked several hundred yards down the road, stopped, and Jenkins appeared to be examining the snow at his feet. After a few minutes he shook his head, turned around and returned to the main highway. This time he walked in the direction of the Easter farm road, the dog sniffing excitedly at his side. At the intersection, he turned and walked south toward Bannah. The road turned sharply, and the men waiting with the truck at the bottom of the hill saw Jenkins stop short, look back toward them and wave both arms over his head. They climbed into the truck, started it and slowly let it climb up the hill toward him, until they were within a few feet. They then stopped, got out and walked over to where Jenkins and the dog were standing.

It appeared to be a little-used road, wheel tracks really, that dipped from the main road off toward the west. Jenkins said nothing, merely pointed to a spot in the snow. The red drops were obvious.

"I can see it!" Whitedeer exclaimed, "there's another spot of blood on down the path there."

The four men and the dog, now straining on her leash, walked carefully in the wheel ruts that led down the path. The procession continued for nearly a quarter mile to where the road dipped and crossed a wooden bridge over a small creek. Huge cottonwood trees lined either side of the bank. When they reached the opposite side of the creek, they could see where the wagon had swerved from the road and gone deeper in among the trees.

"I think we've found the place," Jenkins said, pointing. There, well hidden from the road among the trees, was obviously where the slaughter had taken place.

Red was surprised at the amount of blood which had been spilled. "My God!" he groaned. "Those poor kids!"

Charles Whitedeer had walked a few paces before the other two men. "I think I've got something here," he said, walking away from where most of the blood seemed to have been spilled. He pointed at the ground. Strickland and the crime scene investigator moved slowly to where Charles stood.

"I see it!" Jerry Singer said and immediately pulled his camera from the bag. Just a little way away from where the horses had obviously stood was a clear boot print. He walked around it and took pictures from every angle.

"But how are we going to preserve it?" Charles asked, looking perplexed.

"That's why we are the big guys with the big bucks," Jerry laughed. He returned to Bill Jenkins' pickup and returned with a large case which he set carefully away from the print.

"What's that?" Red asked with interest.

"Watch and learn," the investigator said with a slight smile. He removed a small primus stove which he lit, and put something into a pan. While it was heating he dug a trough that began a little ways away from the boot print at the highest angle and down almost to the beginning of the print. Now all three men stood watching, fascinated, as Jerry removed the pan from the stove and immediately set it in the snow and began stirring the contents. Before they could ask any further questions he picked up the pan and poured the contents into the trough which immediately flowed into the print and solidified.

"What the hell!" Strickland exclaimed, "what is that stuff?"

Jerry carefully cut an area around the print and lifted the entire section. "It's molten sulfur," he explained. "It was cold enough for this to work. You heat it, then cool it until crystals just begin to form and immediately pour it into the print. It makes a perfect cast. The only problem is you only get one shot at it. I think we did it right this time."

"What I'm wondering," Bill Jenkins said as they once again returned to the most trampled areas, "is how did the killer or killers get here. That's the only print I've seen."

"He . . . they . . . could have ridden in on the wagon with the kids and walked out in the packed wagon rut," Red said, thinking out loud. He carefully began removing the blood-stained snow and putting it in plastic evidence bags. "We'll get blood types off this though I don't know how in hell we'll separate them once this damned snow melts."

Bill Jenkins sprinted for the pickup and returned in a few minutes with a Styrofoam cooler. "How about packing some clean snow around all the bags you collect from here," he suggested. "That should keep your blood snow frozen until you can get it processed."

"Good thinking!" the crime scene investigator said and slapped Jenkins on the back.

Red stood staring up at the sky which after showing such a promising sunrise was now quickly becoming overcast. "What I'm still wondering is how did he . . . or they . . . overpower the kids? If it was just one person, he couldn't have held off six healthy kids without some kind of a struggle."

"He could have held them at gun point and made them undress and tie each other up," Bill Jenkins guessed.

Strickland nodded. "Still, he or they would have had to have been following the kids for some time."

"Not necessarily," Jerry Singer supplied. "Maybe those kids just happened to be at the wrong place at the wrong time."

"No way," said Charles Whitedeer. "This was planned and damned well planned at that. The only thing is . . . I don't think they thought about the horses maybe heading for home on their own. Maybe it's someone who doesn't know a lot about horses."

Charles Whitedeer was Native American, a Sioux who had spent most of his growing up years with foster families in Bannah, but had also returned, from time to time, to the reservation. When he had finally decided to try his way in the white man's world, he had been hired as deputy by Red Strickland. He had been working in that capacity now for nearly five years. He and his seventeen-year-old sister, Paula, lived just at the edge of Bannah proper. Paula was also a senior at the high school this year. She had attended grade school at the Indian school and since leaving the reservation to live with Charles, had kept house for him as well as maintaining better than average grades. Still, Charles felt he really didn't know his slim, dark-haired, dark-eyed little sister. Now he sighed in relief that she had not been one of the students who had been along on the hay ride.

Charles had worried about Paula since her moving to Bannah. She, he felt, kept much too much to herself. She was a rather shy girl, but that was not the real problem. Charles felt that Paula would have been a very popular girl if she had allowed people to get closer to her. She studied, was polite and friendly, but in a distant way. He had seen the kids come to the house from time to time, but the same kids didn't seem to want to come back again.

"Don't you want friends, Paula?" he had asked in exasperation one evening after Paula had turned down an invitation to a birthday party. "Don't you get tired of just sitting around the house?"

Paula had shaken her head as she cleared the table. "I don't belong," she had said.

"Not as long as you keep acting like this," Charles had put in, following her to the kitchen.

"That's not what I mean," she said, beginning to run water into the sink as she scraped the remains of their supper into the dog's dish. "Here, Prince!" she called, as the gangly Beagle puppy came eagerly to his supper. "I don't just mean at school . . . I don't know where I belong as a person."

He had understood, or at least had thought he understood her. Sometimes he too felt he was in a no-man's land between his heritage and the world of the white man. "You have to decide sooner or later, you know," he had finally said.

"I don't see gangs of friends beating their way to our door after you either," Paula had shot back, slamming things onto the cabinets. "Just how many people can you count as friends?"

Charles had sighed and picked up a dish towel. "There might be things I'd change if I could, Sis," he admitted, "but I have at least made my peace with myself. You need to do that too."

His reverie was interrupted by the sheriff. "I think I might have found something here." The other men walked over to where he was and he pointed to the ground near a rock. There, lying on the snow, was what looked like a coat button. The button was large and covered in what appeared to be brown corduroy, more than likely to match the coat.

"Good god!" Charles exclaimed. "That looks like the same material . . ."

Red Strickland laid his finger across his lips and shook his head. "I don't remember a corduroy coat like that in the pile of stuff. We'll go through all the clothing again though just to make sure. Now we need to get pictures of this area before the weather messes us up."

Jerry Singer busied himself with the camera he had brought. He carefully photographed the button from several angles as well as the marks in the snow around the blood and horse tracks. Then he carefully scooped the button into a small plastic bag he took from his pocket, sealed the top and made a notation on the bag with his pen. He placed the bag in a compartment of one of the cases he had brought, returned the pen to his pocket and put the camera back in its case. "Ready," he said, turning back to the three men waiting for him.

After that, the four began their walk back to the main road. However, before they had gone a hundred yards, the glowering sky began to rid itself of huge snow flakes. The wind began to pick up and by the time they reached the truck, it was plain that whatever evidence might have been at the crime scene would soon be covered by another heavy blanket of snow.

"Even the weather is against us," Red Strickland muttered, as Ginger was returned to the cage with the other dogs and the gear repacked in the vehicle. The men climbed in ready to start back. "But the bastard has to have made some mistake."

VI

Penny was awakened by the shrilling of the telephone. When she looked at her bedside clock, she was surprised to find that it was already past 10:00 a. m. Vaguely she remembered thinking she had heard the telephone ring sometime earlier. It had been dark and she had fallen back to sleep almost immediately.

There were two telephones in the Strickland home, one in Red's bedroom, the other was a wall phone in the kitchen. Sure that the phone would stop ringing before she could reach either, Penny took her time getting her crutch and making her way down the hall.

She was surprised that the phone was still ringing when she reached it. "Hello," she answered it as she pulled out a chair and eased herself down on it. "Wait till I get my leg propped up somewhere. OK, I got it. What's up?"

"Have you heard?" Betsy Klein's shrill voice from the phone receiver shattered the morning stillness.

"Heard what?" Penny asked, getting herself comfortable. *Betsy, chief gossip and story teller,* she groaned to herself. *This could take awhile.* She wondered what Betsy's latest story would be. "Heard what, Betsy?"

"The kids on the hay ride are all dead!"

"Oh sure! Come on, Betsy, if this is your idea of a joke, it really isn't funny."

"I'm not telling a story this time, Penn," Betsy denied. "The bodies are all at the hospital. They brought them in a couple of hours ago!"

Penny still could not grasp the possibility that what Betsy was saying was true. "Was it an accident?" she asked.

"No!" Betsy almost shattered the phone, her voice had become shriller in her excitement. "They were murdered!"

"Jim, Tracy, Sandy . . ." Penny whispered. "Please, Betsy, tell me this is a sick joke!"

"Didn't your dad tell you?" Betsy demanded.

"Dad's not been here for awhile, I guess," Penny said. "I don't know when he went out, but I just woke up when you called."

"My dad says it's devil worshipers," Betsy now went on. Betsy's father worked for the post office; and, like his daughter, was known to seek followers by way of the tidbits of gossip he was able to pick up and pass on here and there. Penny didn't set much stock by Betsy's opinions or her father's for that matter.

"Bets, I've got to go . . . er . . . there's someone at the door," Penny lied as she hung up the receiver. She sat at the table, chin in hand, and stared out at the darkening sky. Surely this was some kind of dream and she would wake to find she was still tucked in her warm bed. But as Boots brushed insistently against her good leg, asking for his breakfast, Penny returned to reality.

VII

By the time the officers had ridden back to the Easter farm with Bill Jenkins, the wind was blowing at near-blizzard force. "What are you going to do about Will Lester?" Charles asked the sheriff as the two men stood by their car.

"No choice about it now," Red Strickland said. "With the button and his jacket, we've got to haul him in and we're going to have to get every pair of boots he's got around and see if any match that print."

"You arresting him for the murders?"

Red shook his head as the two men approached the outside stairway leading to Will Lester's apartment. "Let's just say I'm going to hold him as a material witness until we get this thing with the jacket and maybe boots straightened out. I'm afraid to leave him here in case he panics and runs."

"Or in case the town people get wind of last night's goings on?"

Red nodded as he rapped sharply on Lester's door.

"What now?" Will Lester sounded almost belligerent as he came to the door, a slight odor showing that he had been augmenting his courage with another bottle. Once again the sheriff and his deputy pushed their way into the small living room. Will Lester studied the faces of the two men and then slowly sank down onto a chair, courage quickly fleeing.

"Sorry to tell you, Will," Red began, "but I've got no choice now but to haul you in to town."

"But why?"

"We found a button at the scene of the murders," Red said, staring hard at the young man. "It bears an awfully strong resemblance to the buttons on the jacket you tried to burn."

"Oh no!" Will Lester paled. "I swear to God, Sheriff . . . I don't even know where the kids were."

Charles Whitedeer walked to the door that led into the minute kitchen and after looking under the sink brought out a large garbage bag. He then went to the bedroom and emerged a few minutes later with the bag filled with every boot, shoe and slipper he had found in the closet, as well as Will's coat. "The weather's getting worse every minute," he said, handing the coat to the still seated Lester. "Hurry now before we can't find our way back to town."

"What's in the bag?" Will Lester demanded, pointing at the bag in Whitedeer's hand.

"We also found a little extra surprise out there," Charles said, "and we just want to see if you might have something that matches it."

"The two of you head for the car," Red said as they all started for the stairs. "I'm going to have a few words with Mr. Easter, and then we'll be ready to go."

"You're gonna make damned sure I don't have a job any more, aren't you," Will Lester demanded. "Or are you hoping they'll lynch me and you won't have to put yourself out any further in finding who really did this?"

"Getting smart-assed about all this isn't going to help your case any," Red said. "The sooner you show some sense and co-operate with us, the sooner you'll be back here on the farm. I'm trying to smooth things for you with Mr. Easter, so just shut up."

It looks like even God isn't on our side," Charles Whitedeer mused, a few minutes later, staring morosely out the side window at the snow as it blew in waves that almost made him seasick. The three of them were driving carefully back to Bannah and the office.

"Hmm," Strickland said, his hands tight on the steering wheel, giving careful concentration to his driving.

"You know, Red, I would have thought lot more than six kids would have gone on that hay ride. They could have crowded a dozen or more kids into that wagon," Whitedeer said, breaking into the silence that had overtaken the three men.

"Billy Singer didn't go 'cause his kid brother is down with the measles. Besides, I don't think he would have gone anyway as I wouldn't let Penny go, and I suppose some of the other Indian kids have probably already gone back to the reservation for the holidays, and a few of the other kids have left for Christmas visits to relatives." Red slowed the car as the snow got even thicker.

"Could be," Whitedeer agreed.

"Jim wanted this first hay ride to be a special one," Will Lester put in from his place in the back seat. "He's been planning it since Thanksgiving, I think."

"I wonder if a bigger crowd of kids would have made a difference?" Charles mused.

"Why didn't Paula go?" Red asked, stopping as a wave of snow blowing across the road temporarily blocked his vision.

"I don't know, she didn't say."

"Want to come by the house for coffee after we drop Will here off at the jail? Somebody's got to break the news to Penny and it would probably be best from me." Somewhat able to see the road again, Red eased the vehicle forward.

"No thanks," Charles said. "Just drop us both off. I can tend to Will and you go on home to Penny. Millie will have the coffee pot on and she probably has her hands full with the phone calls and all that are coming in. You know, Red, I hate it that this damned blizzard has come up, but, at the same time, it might at least keep the reporters off our backs for a while."

There were knots of people gathered in front of various places of business as the sheriff's vehicle entered Bannah's Main Street. At the bank they turned left, and proceeded into the parking lot of the county courthouse which also housed the Sheriff's office and jail.

"Come on, Will," Charles said as he got out of the car and opened the back door. "We'll get you all settled and then see about the evidence."

Will Lester slid across the seat and stepped into the deepening snow. "What if . . . what if they try and come for me?" he whispered.

"You're not being held on any charges, at least not for now," Red reminded him. "With any luck you'll be out of here before anyone knows you're here."

Red pretended he did not see the group of men who were hurrying toward him. He put the car in gear and backed rapidly out of the parking space. He wondered how he would break the news to his daughter. As he drove the short distance home, he thought of the six young lives who wouldn't celebrate Christmas, wouldn't graduate from high school and wouldn't go on to live out their dreams. These were kids who had been in and out of his home since Penny was a little girl. He had umpired their little league games, had attended their plays and concerts, their football and basketball games. He'd also had quiet little talks with Brad Richards and Ted Campbell when he had discovered a little weed in their cars. He'd tried to caution the girls together with his daughter about things they should try to steer clear of. He didn't know what job was harder, being the sheriff or being a parent.

VIII

Strickland entered the front hall, stamping the snow from his boots. He slipped them off there and padded on to his bedroom. He opened his closet and hung up his gun belt on a hook he had on the back of the door where it was easily available and his coat on a hanger. He slipped into the bathroom and splashed some water on his face. God he was tired! But he knew he still had to face Penny.

He could smell bacon frying as he walked down the hallway toward the kitchen. Mrs. Cooley did not come in on weekends. She had offered to when Penny had broken her leg, but Penny had assured her she would be able to manage their meals and what little housework could not be put off until the beginning of the week. He entered the kitchen to find his daughter sitting on a bar stool with her cast leg resting on a second. She was trying to turn bacon in the electric skillet which sat on the butcher block kitchen counter. She turned and met his gaze and he knew that he did not have to tell her the grim news.

"If you'll make the toast, Daddy and pour the coffee, I'll scramble some eggs for you as soon as I get this bacon crisp."

For a little while the pair busied themselves with breakfast preparations. When the table had been set at last and the meal had been dished up they sat across from one another, neither really feeling like eating. Boots sat beside Red's chair, opening his mouth in a silent plea for a bite. Absently Red broke off bits of bacon and dropped them to the cat.

"Who told you, Penny?"

"Betsy, she called about 10:00 this morning."

Strickland shook his head. "I might have guessed," he said.

"Daddy. . .how?"

"Let's get breakfast out of the way and then we'll talk about it, Kitten," Strickland said as he broke off a piece of toast and spread it with orange marmalade. Then he laid both the knife and piece of toast on his plate, feeling a lump rise in his throat that he knew food could never get past.

Penny stared at her plate and moved her eggs around with her fork.

"You've got to eat something, Honey," Red admonished. "You'll feel better with something warm in your stomach."

"I don't really think I'll ever feel better," Penny said. She gazed out of the window and watched the swirls of snow. Their old house was well built and cozy, but already frost was making its way up the insides of the windows.

After breakfast was finished and Penny had scraped most of what had been cooked into the garbage disposal and the dishes had been started in the dishwasher, the two of them went into the living room.

Penny propped herself up on the couch and turned to her father who had settled across the room in his own chair. "Now, Daddy," she said, expectantly.

Red sighed. "Penny," he began," you are going to hear lots of rumors in the next few days. Unfortunately, whatever rumors might be spread can't possibly be worse than the real thing. I'm going to tell you something, because I know you can be trusted to keep your mouth shut. I also want you to think of anything you can tell me about any teachers, kids at school, anything that might help me with this puzzle."

Penny's face reddened and blanched in turns as her father told her what he knew so far about the murders. "So you see," he concluded, "I don't know if this button belongs to one of the victims or not. If you know anyone who wears a brown corduroy coat, tell me."

Penny shook her head. "I'll think about it some, Daddy," she said, "but right now I can't take it all in."

"Can you think of anyone at school who might have had a grudge against those kids?" Red questioned.

"Not really," Penny said. "Oh, Daddy!"

"Yes?"

"There is Donald Bennett," she said excitedly.

"Who's he?"

"He's not in school . . . well, not exactly anyway . . . he and his mom live out of town a ways. Mrs. Cooley gets our fresh eggs and some of our summer vegetables from Donald's mom. He's older, I don't know just how old. Anyway, he dropped out of school a long time ago. I think he had some kind of nervous breakdown. He was in the mental hospital in Jamestown or somewhere. Last fall he started back to school. He hoped he could graduate this year."

"And?"

"Well, about a month ago he missed some pretty simple questions on a English test and when we . . . er . . . the kids laughed at him. He got real mad, jumped up and grabbed Miss Christman by the shoulders and shook her really hard. Said she had made the test really hard just to get him."

"Get him?"

"That was what he said. We thought Miss Christman was going to faint or something. She got real white and sent Jim for Mr. Tuttle."

"What did Mr. Tuttle do?"

"He told Donald he was expelled," Penny said. "Then Donald packed up his books and said he wasn't coming back. But he also said he'd get us one way or another for thinking we were so smart."

Red took a serious look at his daughter on the couch. "I hope you weren't one of the kids who laughed," he said. Penny's cheeks flamed and he didn't have to hear her answer. "Well, it's something to look into. I'll have a talk with Donald and his mother. I have to get back to the office now. Will you be alright? Shall I call Mrs. Cooley to come over and stay with you?"

"No, Daddy, I'll be alright. The kids will be calling about this and I should at least be here to listen. I will think about what you said and see who else I think might be involved."

IX

Charles Whitedeer, with Will Lester in tow, entered the sheriff's office as Red Strickland pulled away from the parking lot. Millie Scott, day-time dispatcher, sat at the radio console table with the phone pressed to one ear. She motioned to the coffee pot with her free hand and at the same time pushed a stack of papers toward the corner of the desk. Whitedeer pulled off his coat and hung it on the hook behind the door. He drew a pad of paper to him, plucked a pen out of its holder and scrawled "I'll be back in a few minutes. I need to go to the cells." After pushing the pad to Millie, he took Will Lester's coat and hung it beside his own. Then he motioned for Will to walk ahead of him. The two men went through a door that led to the basement of the courthouse where the jail cells were located.

"I'm sorry we have to lock you up, Will," Whitedeer said as he opened the door to the first of three cells that ran along the west wall of the basement. All three cells, up to this time, were empty.

"When the town gets wind of the fact that I'm on parole," Will Lester said, "I guess I'm just as happy to be here."

"You know you're only a material witness for now," Whitedeer said, closing the cell door and locking it. "I hope you're misjudging the town and we aren't holding you because we're scared you'll be hurt. Red just wants to make sure you don't make another unauthorized trip out of town."

Will Lester sank down onto the bunk and put his head between his hands. "I got nothing to hide," he said through his fingers. "I'd never hurt those kids or anyone else either."

"I'll have them bring you some lunch down after while," Charles said. "Anything special you'd like?"

"You mean like the last meal the condemned man gets?" Lester said a bit sarcastically.

The deputy didn't bother to answer, just shook his head and returned upstairs. The sheriff's office was a long room which ran back from the front door. The dispatcher's desk sat immediately to the right of the door, with a gray, steel filing cabinet behind it. It was on this cabinet that the automatic coffee maker sat with its attendant tray of powdered cream and sugar as well as the mugs belonging to the department's crew. A door at the rear of the room led to the small private office belonging to the sheriff.

As Charles returned from locking Lester in a cell, Millie swiveled her chair to face him. "This phone hasn't stopped ringing since I got here this morning," she sighed, as she set the receiver back on its cradle none too gently. "I still can't take it all in. What's the deal with Lester anyway?"

Charles sat down at his desk and began paging through the stack of papers she had handed him previously. "Red's holding him as a material witness for right now," he said.

"Why, do you think he killed the kids?"

"Hard to say. He pulled some pretty stupid stuff. He found the bodies and then . . . well, Red can fill you in if he wants to."

"Was it . . . ah . . . as bad as what I've heard?"

"It's pretty gory, all right," Whitedeer said. He pulled the phone to him and began to dial his home number. "Paula," he said after a minute, *"Me* . . . Have you heard? Yes, it's all true . . ." He listened a moment then replied, "I'll be home when you see me . . . Yeah, we'll be working double shifts on this one for sure. Be thinking of anything you know or hear that could help us, Hon."

Laying the phone back on its cradle, Whitedeer picked up the stack of papers and began glancing at their messages. "News sure travels fast," he muttered as he flipped through the sheets.

"Especially bad news," Millie agreed.

"I guess the first thing we'll need to do is talk with those kids' parents. Guess that is something I better wait for Red on and we can go together."

"What do you want me to do about the news media?" Millie asked.

"Tell them we are still investigating, and Sheriff Strickland will have a statement for them presently, or words to that effect. We'll leave any details for Red to decide."

As his name was spoken, the sheriff walked into the office, flipping his hat in the doorway of his private office to land, as usual, at the edge of his desk. It had never slid all the way across and off but there was a standing pool in the office that said it would. No winner so far.

Whitedeer rose from his chair. "The vultures are swooping," he commented. "We'd better get out of here before they all land."

Red stepped to the coffee pot and poured a cup, his fifteenth he figured since he got up that morning. "I think our best plan of action will be to find out just where those kids went last night and who they might have seen," he said as he sipped from the cup.

"Want me to come with you, or shall we split up?"

"You take half the list and I'll take the other," Red said. "We can keep in touch on the car radios if we come across anything."

"Every scanner in town will be on and tuned," Charles objected. "Do you want the people to know what we know before we even know it?"

Red sighed and rubbed his chin in agitation. "What they don't know they'll make up anyway. But tell you what, put letters by each of your names and I will do the same, that way we can refer to the subjects by code letter. Won't hide it for long, but best I can do right now."

He turned toward the dispatcher's desk. "Anything else I need to know or do before we hit the streets again?"

Millie briefly summarized what she and Whitedeer had discussed about reporters and the public and Red approved the chief deputy's suggestions. He grabbed a pad and pencil on her desk and quickly jotted a statement about how the investigation was continuing and he would have a public statement later. He tossed the pad to her and, turning, said, "That won't hold them for long but it is the best I can do for now. Do the best you can, Millie and hold the fort. Oh, probably need to keep the coffee pot hot too; see you!" He grabbed his hat from the desk, and slamming it on his head, went through the door that Charles was holding open.

Red Strickland parked in front of Sam Tuttle's house. It would be a good place to start, to find out any school problems the kids had as well as getting a different idea about each of the students. Red thought he knew them all pretty well after having been sheriff as long as he had. But a second opinion always helped and since Tuttle had been the high school principal almost as long as Red could remember, his opinion should count.

The house was imposing and sat on the highest hill in town where it could *oversee,* at least that was how Red thought of it, the goings on of the community and its inhabitants. The family had been quite prominent in Bannah society and Sam Tuttle had been an only child, born when his parents had despaired of there ever being a child. He had been given all the advantages possible from a well-to-do farming couple.

When he had graduated from Jamestown Teachers College and decided to return to Bannah as school teacher, his parents were extremely disappointed. They had hoped for better and higher ambitions from their son. A school teacher was not their idea of a suitable job for a Tuttle.

As the years had passed and his parents had passed on, Sam had made a permanent place for himself in the educational system. Now, nearing sixty, he had already overseen the education of one Bannah generation and was now looking after the growing-up years of another.

Strickland knew that the kids had all nicknamed Sam Tuttle, "Sam Turtle." It did seem somewhat appropriate. Tuttle was a short, round, little man with a rosy, round face and a constant droll expression. He had been nearly bald since he was just a young man and had a habit of pulling his already short neck deep into his collar when speaking to anyone. Now, as he met the sheriff at the door and ushered him into a large, old-fashioned living room, he did rather give the appearance of a turtle either just pulling into or emerging from its shell.

"Come in Sheriff Strickland, I rather expected you to call. Such a sad occasion! Can I get you some coffee or something stronger?" he asked, taking the Sheriff's hat and coat and hanging them on an old style coat rack just inside the door, and motioning Red to a chair.

"No thank you," Red said, settling himself in the indicated over-stuffed chair. "I came to pick your brain. You know almost everyone who lives in Bannah. Can you think of any reason why those kids should have been murdered or anyone who might have been carrying some kind of grudge against any one of them?"

Sam Tuttle sat on the edge of his own chair, hands resting on knees, with a sad, solemn expression on his almost baby face. "I've been thinking of nothing else since the news broke," he said. "They were all good kids. Oh, I won't say the boys didn't do a little nipping and smoking in the locker room; or, for that matter, that all the girls involved were still virgins; but for the most part, they were good kids."

Red tried to hide a smile at the principal's stuffy view of his pupils. "Do you think it was one or several other kids?"

"There are rumors about Satan worshipers in the area," Tuttle offered. "Could it have been something like that?"

"I somehow don't think so. Where were you Friday evening?" Strickland asked, getting to his feet and walking to the large bay window that overlooked the town. "Did the kids happen to come up this way caroling?"

"As a matter of fact," Tuttle admitted, "they did. You know the final exams were taken this past week. I was busy grading some of the papers and I heard the kids singing as they rode up the hill."

"Did they stop here?" Red asked.

Tuttle nodded. "Yes, they did, I invited them in for cookies and hot chocolate."

"How did they seem?"

"Great. They were in high spirits and fine voice. They spent about twenty minutes here with the chocolate and cookies; some of them tried to get me to tell them how they had done on their tests."

Red turned from the window. He wondered that Tuttle had been so friendly with the kids. From what he had heard, Tuttle was a near recluse when he was not teaching. He had few friends in town and kept mostly to himself, another thing to check. "If you think of anything else or hear anything, please get in touch with us."

Tuttle assured him that he would, and getting his hat and coat for him, escorted him to the door.

"Oh," Red said, turning back to the principal. "You could do me a big favor. Call all the teachers who are still in town as well as the senior class members. I want to see them in the study hall this evening. Perhaps by then someone will have thought of something useful."

"Most of the high school teachers are probably still in town as there were some students having to do make up tests. I'll do as you ask and schedule for . . . what? Maybe 6 o'clock?"

"Sounds fine," Red said. Then almost as an afterthought he asked, "Can you give me an idea of the coats and jackets you have around here?"

Tuttle pulled his neck even further into the collar of his shirt as he eyed the sheriff. "I can't name all of them for sure. I think I have a dark blue overcoat and a light blue jacket…er…maybe a gray coat or two, and of course the suit coats and jackets I wear for school. Why do you ask?"

"Just checking, anyway thanks for the help and I will see you at the meeting," Strickland said, slipping into his own navy blue coat and walking out the front door.

"Unit Two, Unit One, you handy?" Red spoke into the microphone of the radio as he started the car and sat for a moment, letting it warm up.

"Right here," Whitedeer replied.

"I've just talked to 'Code Alpha,'" Red said. "He said the kids stopped at his place last night."

"Hmm," Charles said.

"What does that mean?"

"No comment," Charles laughed. "Not much on mine as yet, let you know details later. I'm headed to 'Code Delta's' place."

"10-4, keep in touch, Unit One clear." Red said and replaced the microphone on its hook.

XI

Lynn Christman lived in a small frame house on Second Avenue just off Main Street. She had been Bannah High School's English teacher for the past two years. She admitted Red Strickland into a neat, well-furnished living room. "I was just making myself a cup of tea," she said, seating him in a comfortable armchair. "Would you care for some?"

"Thanks if it's not too much trouble," Strickland said. He was not really fond of tea, but felt he would possibly get Miss Christman more relaxed if she had something to do. "I can join you in the kitchen," he offered.

"Oh no," she said, "that won't be necessary. I will just be a few minutes."

As he waited, Red looked around the orderly little room with appreciation. One wall was filled with shelves containing numerous books; some looked new in bright jackets, others had a well-read, older look. The top shelves were filled with tiny cups and saucers and gaily decorated porcelain boxes. He got up to examine the books. He was surprised to note what appeared to be a number of horror and mystery type books occupying shelf space.

"Here we are," Lynn Christman said, as she returned to set a tray of tea things and a small plate of cookies on the coffee table. "I see you are admiring my books."

"Quite the collection, are you a mystery fan?" Red asked with a smile as he accepted the cup she handed him. "No, thank you, this is fine." He waved off the sugar bowl she was offering to him.

Lynn seated herself, balancing her own tea cup in its saucer on the arm of a chair opposite his. "Yes, but unfortunately," she said, "all my reading is of little use when it comes to trying to puzzle out what happened Friday night."

"I know thinking about it is difficult but can you think of anyone in or out of the school setting who might want to kill those kids," Red asked, taking a sip from his cup. Then he set it on the end table beside his chair and leaned back, prepared to devote all his attention to her words.

"They were all just normal kids," Lynn Christman said. "I'm glad Penny and Paula were not among them." she added almost shyly.

"I wouldn't let Penny go because of the broken leg. That cast wouldn't have been the easiest thing to haul aboard a wagon." Red said. "I guess Paula had other plans."

"Yes, Paula is a very serious student," Lynn said, rising to offer more tea, which Red refused with a motion of his hand. After refilling her own cup, she turned back to her chair and continued, "She and Penny are so, well, so different in their personalities, and yet they are my two best students. Wish I had a dozen more like them."

"There just seems no reason for this, no handle on the case." Red admitted. "Six healthy, normal kids go on a hay ride and then are . . ." He let his voice trail off as a picture of the carnage on the hay wagon came to his mind.

"Do you think it was some other students, someone with a grudge or someone who was jealous?" Lynn asked.

"I doubt it," Red said. "It was too well planned. There is something . . . a clue of sorts . . . but I'm not at liberty to discuss it right now." He stood and began to pace the small room. "The snow storm botched any real investigation at the murder scene," he complained. "What we can't puzzle out is how the killer got the kids to the murder spot or how he left it. Both his clothes and whatever vehicle he might have used would have been… er…pretty messed up . . ." His voice trailed off as he realized that anyone and everyone in Bannah, even Lynn Christman, could well be his killer.

Lynn appeared not to notice his pause. "He couldn't have worn the murder clothes afterward either, if what I have heard is the case. With the blood and stuff, he would have needed a change of clothing."

Red ran his fingers through his hair. "That's a thought," he admitted. "two sets of clothing, one for the slaughter, one to put on afterward for the trip home, or wherever. Did you happen to see the kids Friday night?"

"Oh yes, they came by and sang carols. As you can see, my house isn't very big. It was really quite overflowing with six bundled up kids and myself in here."

"Did they act strange or say anything?"

"No, they were so happy to be out of school for two weeks. I think some of the boys had been nipping a little to keep themselves warm," she smiled up at Red. "Maybe the girls too. I gave them cupcakes and hot chocolate. Jim Easter asked if he could add a little brandy to his." She looked sad as she remembered the scene. "'Medicinal to keep from catching his death of cold,' was what he said." Tears began to trickle down her pale, oval face.

Red Strickland felt constrained to put a hand on her shoulder, why he didn't know, perhaps to comfort her? *Funny,* he thought. He hadn't really paid any attention to her before. She was a strange, somehow out-of-place person living all alone. "I know how you feel. I think this is enough for now. If you think of anything else, please call me either at the office or at home."

She pulled away and brushed at the tears with the back of her hand. "It just doesn't make any sense," she said, walking him to the door.

On the porch he turned and looked back at her. "Maybe when all this is over . . . dinner or something?" he began, then tipped his hat and walked to his car.

After the car had backed from the driveway, Lynn Christman carried the tray of tea and untouched cookies into the kitchen, poured herself another cup and sat at the table, musing, as the tea cooled, untouched, before her. Penny's father was a nice enough man, she guessed, but she really couldn't get involved with anyone, could she? It had been a long time since she had allowed herself to think of a man in that way. Other arms around her? Other lips? No, out of the question! He was all she needed, all she had ever needed. It would not do to arouse his jealousy!

Driving carefully down the street, Red thought about the visit he had just made. He was still turning her over in his mind. Lynn Christman didn't really appear to be the type of person who would be interested in or even at home with dainty things. She was of average height but her figure was spare and gave the appearance of a boy. Her blond hair was cut short and worn straight. She wore little makeup and when not in class generally appeared in jeans and shirts. To Red she looked more like the type who would be at home on a horse or in the out-of-doors. Perhaps all those little things had been handed down from her mother, another thing to look into. Red wanted to know more about her, he decided, and not entirely because of the murders. He wanted to know about her background, from where she came, her family and just everything. Then he returned his attention to the task at hand. There were still so many people to see. He guessed he would make a stop at the nursing home next.

XII

While Red was musing over Lynn Christman, Charles Whitedeer had driven to the condominium owned by William Hein, Bannah's history teacher, and Leonard Jacobs, Bannah's only pharmacist. Hein had taught history at Bannah High School since graduating from teachers college.

I wonder why he decided to come here, Charles asked himself as he approached the door. A few moments after the bell sounded deep in the house's interior, the door was opened by Hein who wore jeans and a *Bannah Tigers* sweat shirt. "I was expecting you, or at least one of you from the Sheriff's office," he said, motioning Charles into the entry hall. "Come on in the living room. Len and I were watching a football game. Can I make coffee or something?"

"No thanks," Charles said as he sat down on a low-backed love seat that was sitting in front of the sliding glass doors that led out onto the small patio in the minute back yard. Leonard Jacobs who sat near the television, was nursing a beer and barely acknowledged his entry.

Hein sat in the other armchair opposite the love seat and raised his eyebrows questioningly. "How can we help?"

"We are going down the route of the hayride asking everyone basically the same questions," Whitedeer said. "Do you know anyone who might have had something against this particular group of kids?"

Hein shook his head. "They weren't the worst or the best kids in school if you know what I mean. All pretty average kids. Jim Easter was one of our best basketball players, as was Ted Campbell and they were both popular."

"Must have been some maniac from out of town," Jacobs put in, setting his beer can down and finally diverting his attention from the action on the television screen. "I've only been in town a few years, you know, since I bought out old man Mason's drug store. Still I think I know most everyone who lives around here; and, frankly, I can't conceive of anyone in town who could do such a thing."

Charles shook his head. "There are circumstances I can't talk about right now that would make that out-of-towner theory seem unlikely. We do feel the kids were known by the person or persons who did this. Did you see the kids last night?"

The two men exchanged glances. "We heard them," Jacobs offered.

"I guess they thought they would disturb the rest of the condo people if they came in," Hein added. "They pulled up in front of our condo and were caroling pretty loudly."

"What time was that, if you noticed?"

"It was pretty early," Hein said, "probably not later than nine or nine-thirty, wouldn't you say so, Leonard?" He looked over at his housemate.

Jacobs nodded in agreement. "It was before the late news came on, I asked them how long they planned to keep the town awake and they said, 'until the sheriff comes and arrests us.'"

"I wish we had," Charles said, getting to his feet. As he reached the door, he turned back to the two men. "By the way, would either of you mind if I have a look in your closets," he asked.

"Not me," Jacobs said, "I don't mind."

William Hein looked startled. "Why would you want to do that?" Both men stared at the deputy. "What if I say no?" Hein asked.

"Do you have any reason to?" Charles asked. "I can get a warrant pretty fast, you know."

Hein smiled grimly. "Put that way," he said, "let's have a look!"

Charles followed the two men into the bedrooms on the upper level. He examined the clothes in both closets and noted that they were all neat and orderly. "Guess you're in luck," he said, leaving the second bedroom. "I don't see anything that fits what we might be looking for. Thanks for your cooperation and you know where I am if you think of anything."

The Chief Deputy had as little luck at his other stops as he had at the two men's home. Several of the teachers admitted to having seen or heard the children drive by, but, at least as far as they would admit, the children had not stopped and left the wagon at their homes.

Whitedeer and Strickland met back at the office. "Well," Strickland asked, "what did you find?"

"Hein and Leonard acted queer," Whitedeer said.

"Was that a pun or an observation?" Strickland asked, keeping a serious expression.

Whitedeer ignored the question. "Hein first made a stink about my checking their closets and clothing but then gave in. No coat."

"I doubt it would be in any shape to hang back in the closet," Red said rather sarcastically. "Although Lynn Christman suggested there could have been a spare coat the killer might have taken along just for that reason."

"He sure would have had to wear something back home," Charles agreed. "Had you thought about checking cars?"

"Not yet," Red admitted. "There's nothing to suggest the killer had the kids anywhere but in and around the hay wagon. If the button was from a second coat, and the more I think about that possibility, the more sense it makes, there wouldn't be any signs of blood in whatever vehicle or vehicles the killer used before killing the kids."

"Guess we could use Jenkins' dogs to check out cars if it comes to that."

"Not a bad thought, verify anything they find with Luminol. We aren't there yet though, I don't even know what cars to search," Red said.

"Back to Hein and Jacobs," Charles said. "Those two guys are neater than they made us be in school, They either did one hell of a job of getting rid of all the evidence before it ever got back to their place, or they didn't have anything to do with it."

"What about boots?" Red asked. "You didn't mention them."

Whitedeer shook his head. "Loafers, running shoes, slippers but not a boot anywhere that I saw."

"Isn't that kind of odd?" Red wondered aloud.

Whitedeer scratched his chin thoughtfully. "I'll check that one out, Chief."

"I hear they are more than friends," Red said, getting himself a cup of coffee and extending the pot to Charles who nodded and held out his mug.

"I've heard that too." Charles sipped from the now hot mug and grimaced. "Time to wash the pot or at least make fresh."

"Who has time? Anyway their relationship could be an angle."

"You mean a proposition turned down?"

Red sighed and stretched his legs out in front of him. "I don't know. Just fishing. I wouldn't think it would be necessary to kill a whole group of kids for a turn down."

"Maybe they were afraid that whoever was propositioned told the other kids," Charles offered. "Maybe they're kinky as well as queer. Remember those two guys, Leopold and Loeb, back in the twenties, who killed a kid just because they wanted to find out what it would be like to kill someone?"

"God," Strickland heaved a sigh, "that's way before my time . . . and yours."

"They made a movie about it," Whitedeer supplied, sinking into his own chair. "I saw it on late-night TV a week or so ago."

"Could have given someone ideas, I guess. But why six kids then?" Strickland wondered.

XIII

Red finished his coffee, got up and put on his hat and headed for the door.

"Where are you going now?" Charles asked, taking their two mugs and rinsing them in the small sink.

"Where I don't want to go, it is time I talked to the families of those poor kids."

"Sure you don't want company?"

Red looked thoughtfully at his deputy and then shook his head. "No, not this time. I feel like this is one of those things I've got to do alone." When he reached the door he turned back and said, "Oh, I almost forgot, I told Sam to arrange a meeting of those teachers and seniors still in town for 6:00 this evening at the school. I know all the parents will want to be there as well."

"Anything I can do to help?" Charles asked as he set the two mugs back on the shelf next to the coffee pot.

"If you don't mind, call Paula and ask if she'd mind taking Penny as I have no idea how long these interviews are going to take."

"I'm on it right now," Charles said, picking up the phone and punching in numbers even as Red was still on his way out the door.

The home of Tracy Wilkins was nearest the Sheriff's office, so Red Strickland pulled his car into the Wilkins driveway and steeled himself for the interview. Mrs. Wilkins opened the door to his ring so quickly that Red knew she had been watching his approach. She took him into the small living room and offered him the big recliner chair that faced the television.

"Mrs. Wilkins," Red began after setting his hat and coat on the floor beside the chair. "I'm so sorry that I have to pay this call on you. I know it isn't a good time but there are things though that I need to know."

Georgia Wilkins perched on the edge of the sofa, like a little bird that would take flight at the least sudden movement. "I understand," she said softly.

Red noted the little Christmas tree on a table in front of the picture window. It was gaily decorated with many small, colorful packages underneath it.

Georgia Wilkins followed his gaze sadly. "Such a waste," she said.

Red knew she was not talking about the packages that now would never be opened by her granddaughter. He cleared his throat, fighting the lump that was forming there. Again he saw Penny, so eager for that hay ride, so angry with him. "Can you think of anyone who would want to harm those kids?" he asked, knowing even as the question left him there was no answer.

Mrs. Wilkins shook her head sadly. "Those were some of the brightest kids in their class," she said. "Tracy was looking forward to going off to school. She wanted to be a veterinarian, you know. She had high hopes of returning to Bannah and settling down with that Campbell boy." Tears welled up in her eyes and she made no move to stop them as they coursed down her cheeks.

Red Strickland walked to where she sat and offered her his handkerchief. "I know this is hard on you, Georgia," he said, seating himself beside her. "If it hadn't been for Penny's broken leg . . ." his voice trailed off.

There was a momentary angry flicker in Georgia Wilkins' eyes, but it was so fleeting Red Strickland was not certain he had seen it or if it had, instead, been his own feelings of guilt at having been spared this tragedy.

"Tracy was a good girl," Mrs. Wilkins said softly. "She came home from school, helped me with the house, and kept up her studies. There was just no reason for it." Then turning fully to face the sheriff, she added, "Please, Red, find the monster who did this . . . for all of us and for all of them!"

"I promise if they are alive to be found, I'll find them," Red said. "But there's something you can do for me if you will."

Georgia looked at him and nodded. "Anything," she whispered.

"I know it's going to be difficult but I want you to go through all of Tracy's things. If she kept a diary or a journal I want you to look for anything that she might have said that might shed some light on this tragedy. If there are any letters or . . . well . . . anything that you're not expecting to find, please read them."

Georgia Wilkins stared at the sheriff uncomprehendingly. "I will," she finally said, "but I don't think there will be anything to find."

Red put his arm around her and held her small body for a few minutes. "We just have to try everything, Georgia," he said.

XIV

He took his leave shortly after that and drove to the Richards home. It was all so useless. He knew that, but still he had to try. Police procedure and his own conscience demanded it. The Richards' living room was large and "lived in." There was a huge Christmas tree with its top nearly touching the high ceiling. It seemed so out of place there under the circumstances.

Mrs. Richards brought in a tray with coffee and cookies, bright with colored sugar and cut into holiday shapes, which she set on the low table in front of the couch. Their two little boys were not in the room. George Richards looked pale and drawn and his wife's eyes were red-rimmed and swollen.

Red accepted the cup of coffee Mrs. Richards handed him. He wondered that people didn't forget hospitality, even in such trying times. But then food had always been an expression, a solace, the thing offered in times of sadness and gladness alike.

"I know what you are going to ask," George Richards said out of the silence. "Martha and I have talked of nothing else since we got the news. There was simply no reason for those kids to have been killed like that."

"Did Brad mention anyone, at school, or people he might have had dealings with in your store, that might have had a grudge against him, against you, against any of those kids?"

Both the Richards shook their heads in negation. "Ordinary kids," George Richards said. "Ordinary kids in an ordinary town, living ordinary lives."

"Anyone jealous of Brad going with Sandy, or Sandy going with Brad for that matter?"

"They were just kids!" Martha Richards burst out. "They would be going with lots of other people before they were ready to settle down."

"You know that and I know that," the sheriff said, settling back in the chair. "But when you're seventeen, you don't know that! Everything is here and now. There is no future, they think they will live forever."

"What does your daughter say?" George Richards asked. "She didn't go . . . she didn't have to die!" he burst out in sudden anger. His hands began to tremble violently and deep color suffused his face.

His wife moved to his side and put a comforting arm around his shaking shoulders. "Please, George," she begged. "This isn't going to help anyone."

Red felt their sadness, their resentment. Perhaps this was the reason he had to make these visits by himself. Their children were dead, his child was alive. "Penny broke her leg a few weeks ago," he said softly. "I wouldn't let her go because of her cast. She was very angry with me . . ."

"I'm sorry," George Richards said, "I should not have said what I did."

Red shook his head. "I understand your feelings, George. Bannah was a quiet little town up until a few years ago," he said, more to himself than to the Richards. "I look at the faces of the people I pass on the street and now wonder if one of them is a murderer."

"You don't think?" Martha Richards gasped. She sank down beside her husband, visibly shaken by the possibility that the killer of her boy was someone they saw every day. "You don't really think it is someone from here, someone we know?" The two Richards exchanged horrified glances. "We thought. . .that is . . . someone outside . . ."

"I want to believe that," Red Strickland said, setting down the cup in his hand. "But it's not likely. The person who did this job knew the kids, knew about the hay ride, and had their confidence."

"How do you know that?" George Richards questioned, grabbing his wife's hand even more tightly.

"I can't tell you that right now," Strickland said. "I'm afraid there is proof though that this person knew at least one of the kids. And now, I've got to ask the two of you to do something for me. I want you to check everything in Brad's room . . . notes, journals, letters, anything that might indicate there was something going on that he was reluctant to talk about with you."

"Brad didn't keep any secrets from us," Mrs. Richards objected. "We always have taught our boys that they can come to us with anything . . . problems . . . anything!"

"I'm sure you're right," Strickland said, getting ready to take his leave. "But please do this for me just on the off chance . . ." He let his words trail off as he turned to the door.

He left the Richards home, brushing angrily at the tears forming in his own eyes. All these families. All these children whose lives had been so vibrant, whose futures had seemed so assured. It was true, no one could predict what might have happened in their futures, other tragedies, but not to seventeen and eighteen-year-olds! He knew the questions he asked their families were probably useless. He hated deepening the wounds that were already there. But he knew he had to continue. There could always be that one thing—that one little clue—a word said, a remembered incident, that might unearth the killer.

The snow was falling again when he pulled up to the Reed house. He was surprised at the sigh of relief that escaped him when there was no answer to his knock. It would have to be gone through later, he knew, but at least for now this was one family he didn't have to face, three pairs of accusing eyes because Penny still lived.

XV

The Nye house, like the Wilkins house, was quiet when Strickland knocked at the door. Kathryn Nye let him in and took him to the kitchen where he sat in the cozy breakfast nook. This was a much lived in part of the house. He could see that from the many little things that were there: a sewing basket, a book with a cat-shaped book mark keeping the page that now would never be turned. A small television sat on a shelf and two chairs were drawn up there in companionable emptiness.

"Kathryn," Red began, taking both her ice-cold hands into his large ones. "I'm so terribly sorry. Penny and Marcia spent so many wonderful times at our house."

Kathryn Nye smiled a shaky little smile. "I know," she said. "Penny and Marcia practiced a lot of cheer leading up in Marcia's room. I thought at times the ceiling would come down with their jumping around." Without warning, she buried her face against his chest and began sobbing uncontrollably. "What am I going to do, Red?" she sobbed. "She was all I had left . . ."

Red stood up and led her gently to one of the corner chairs. "Sit here," he said. "I'll get the coffee." He reached cups from the cupboard and filled them from the coffee maker that sat full and hot on the immaculate counter. "I'm making the rounds of the parents," he said lamely, setting the coffee cups down on the table between the two chairs. "Can you think of anything, jealousy, a grudge, something Marcia might have said?"

Kathryn shook her head. "Marcia got on well with everyone," she said. "She liked her teachers, and they all liked her too. She got good grades, kept up her school work and wanted to go on to nursing school this fall."

"Did you see the kids in town at all after they went on the hay ride?" Red asked.

Kathryn shook her head. "I didn't think they were going to come into town."

"They sang carols at the old folks' home," Red said. "They also stopped in at some of the teachers' houses. I thought they might have stopped by to see Penny; but then . . ." he picked up his cup and sipped at the steaming liquid. "I guess they knew how upset she was to miss it . . ." He dropped his gaze and studied his finger nails. He dreaded seeing that accusation he was sure would be in Kathryn's eyes. "There is some evidence . . . something I can't tell you right now," he said. "Please keep your ears open though for me if you will."

"What am I looking for?" Kathryn questioned.

"I don't know," Red admitted. "There has got to be something . . . something involving one or more of those kids. No one does what was done for no reason."

"Do you mean someone hated one or more of those children enough to . . . to . . ." her voice trailed off and she buried her face in her hands. "Why not simply single out that person?" Her question was muffled through hands that still covered her face. She raised horrified eyes to look deep into Red's. "What kind of fiend would sacrifice innocent lives for a . . . a . . . grudge?"

Red stood abruptly and gathered Kathryn into his arms. "I don't know," he murmured against her dark hair, "but if I have to, I'll die trying to find out."

"I know you will," she said. "I thank God that Penny was . . . is . . . safe." Her generosity was overwhelming. For a long moment they clung together, each attempting to give and receive some measure of comfort. "Tell Penny to come see me when she is able," Kathryn finally said, releasing the sheriff and looking up into his face. "There are things that Marcia would have wanted her to have."

Red pulled a handkerchief from his pocket as he cleared his throat. He blew his nose unashamedly. "I'll tell her," he promised. "I know she will want to . . ." Kathryn had led into what he was about to ask so he turned to her, not quite knowing how to frame his request. "Kathryn," he began, "if you could look at all of Marcia's things for me . . . maybe she kept a journal or a diary, maybe there were letters; just anything that might give us some insight into things she might not have been willing to share with you or want to worry you."

Kathryn raised her eyes to his in horror. "You don't really think," she whispered, "that there might have been something she could have told me that could have prevented all this!"

"At this point I'm just not willing to leave anything to chance," Red admitted.

After Kathryn Nye's husband had died, Red had often thought that perhaps beginning a relationship with her would be a comfortable and comforting thing to do. They were, after all, both alone with daughters who behaved much as sisters might. But there had always been so much work, so little time. Now, he promised himself, when this was all over, he would come back and try to help heal the sorrow that Kathryn was suffering.

By the time that Red got to his car and opened the door, the snow was falling again very heavily. *Scratch the trip to the Campbell and Easter farms right now,* he thought, and felt relieved. He really did not feel up to that quite yet. It was an unprofessional feeling, he knew and was glad none of the deputies knew. But he remembered seeing the Campbell family in town, Ted, his two little sisters tagging behind him like puppies, treating them to a Saturday matinee. The entire Campbell family entering or leaving church together. There had been so much love there. He slammed his fist down on the steering wheel in frustration. There had to be some clue to the killer's identity. More than anything he wanted the satisfaction of putting that fiend where he belonged. But there was also the nagging fear that the killer could be someone he'd known for years. What then? So lost in thought was he that he was surprised to see how deeply the snow had piled against the windshield. Cursing, he got out and scraped away the snow and then returned to his office; he and his chief deputy spent the rest of the afternoon fielding phone calls until time to close the day shift.

XVI

"Wonder if Doc has finished the autopsies yet," Charles said, as the two men drove away from the sheriff's office.

"Stop by the hospital," Red said. "The causes of death are pretty obvious. We'll have to wait for the crime lab to come up with anything special, I guess."

At the hospital they were confronted with knots of people standing in the waiting room. Red frowned, and raising his voice, said, "All right, all of you can go home. There is nothing to be gained by hanging around here. When there is something to tell we will tell those of you who need to know."

Before he could say more, reporters with microphones and cameramen surrounded him and his deputy. "Is it true Satan worshipers did this?" demanded a shrill-voiced, frizzy blonde reporter from Channel 23 in Bismarck.

"Who were the victims?" It was a burly man Red recognized from a station in Fargo.

"What can you tell us about the cause of death?" a tall, red-headed woman shouted, elbowing her way through the knot of reporters and attempting to grasp Red's arm.

"No comment!" Red barked, pulling away from the woman. "All of you clear out of here, please. There are sick people in this hospital. We don't know anything yet. When we find out something we'll hold a news conference, not before."

"Is it true you can't handle this investigation on your own," the red-head persisted. "We hear the State Crime Lab as well as police from all over the state are going to be here to help you."

Red shook her off once again. Turning to her with ice in his eyes, he said, "I'll be happy for any help anyone offers. I'll also let *you* see the inside of one of our cells if you don't keep your hands off me!"

Silence fell in the crowded waiting room. Red surveyed each of the reporters and his expression told them that he would stand for no nonsense. Silently the milling men and women filed from the room.

Dr. Harden appeared at the door of his office and motioned the two men inside.

As Red and Charles pulled chairs near his desk and sat, Dr. Harden picked up a fat folder that had been lying on his desk. "I never saw such a mess," he sighed. "I took samples of everything I could think of and the state boys have already headed back for Bismarck with them and a copy of my report. I told them to give you a call no matter what time of day or night they came up with anything that might help us. Hope you don't mind. This is the original for you." He thrust the folder toward the sheriff.

"With this storm out there, I wonder how long it will take them to get back to Bismarck and start on the samples," Strickland said, accepting the folder and placing it on the arm of the chair in which he sat. "I'll read this later. Just give us a summary now."

The doctor picked up a pen and began doodling on the blotter on his desk. "I can give you most of it in a nutshell," he said. "The kids were all healthy enough, no problems with hearts, lungs, kidneys, etc. The kids had been well-nourished and well-developed. There was no sign of beginning arterial disease. For all intents and purposes, it appears these were pretty clean-living kids. No sign of drug use, legal or illegal. That's all the bodies can tell us for now, until the report gets back from Bismarck."

"Did you come up with anything at all that might help?" Red asked.

Harden dropped the pen and stared directly at the Sheriff. "What about yourself? Anything to share with me?"

Red had known the doctor for a long time and felt no compunction about sharing his thoughts with him. "Nothing really; Penny came up with one possible lead." Red proceeded to tell the other two men Penny's story about Donald Bennett.

"What do you think, Charles?" Harden asked, peering over his glasses at the deputy who had remained silent throughout the entire conversation.

"Hard to tell," Whitedeer responded. "You can't crawl into someone else's brain, can you?"

"Ha! Psychiatrists claim to do it all the time!" The doctor gave a short snort of laughter, then looked seriously at them from across his desk. "What is Donald doing now, is he in trouble?"

"Not really. I guess he stays pretty much around home. We deal with his mom some for eggs and fresh vegetables, but I don't think I've seen Donald personally more than three or four times." Red settled back in the chair.

"I had to send him to Jamestown for commitment a few years ago," Harden said. "He got pretty agitated and started making threats toward his mother. She finally asked me if I would consider getting commitment forms. Donald decided he wanted to be committed voluntarily. I think he realized he was getting out of control. Sure saved some paperwork and time in court."

"What's his problem?" Charles asked, getting to his feet, removing his coat and slinging it across the back of the chair.

"That's not a bad idea," Strickland said, relieving himself of his own bulky jacket.

"If you two gentlemen are through making yourselves more comfortable," the doctor said with a broad wink, "I'll go on with my story about Donald. The staff at Jamestown says he suffers from an extreme nervous condition as well as chronic depression. I also think sitting out there in the country being consumed with *Smother's Love* doesn't help the situation either."

Strickland raised his eyebrows. *"Smother's Love?"*

Harden grinned. "Combination of *smother* and *mother*, my own diagnosis. It's a term I made up for overly protective moms who feel they have to shield their kids from life's ups and downs. All they end up doing is depriving their kids of any kind of a normal life at all."

"Wonder what you'd call a smothering father?" Red smiled grimly. "I'm sure that's what Penny thinks I am."

Harden and Whitedeer both smiled. Any attempt at lightness at this juncture was appreciated even if it was a bit flat.

"Anything else you can think of before we leave, Doc?" Strickland asked.

"Don't think so," Hardin said. "The kill seems to have been the thrill. There does seem to be one other possibility."

The chief deputy, who had once again put on his coat and already opened the door and started out, turned back with his hand on the knob. "What's that?" He and Strickland asked in unison.

"I really don't want to be speaking out of turn until the lab gets its results back to you but I think the kids could have been drugged."

"What makes you suspect drugs?" Strickland sat back down in the chair, and Whitedeer closed the door again softly.

The doctor began to speak again. "The kids had a couple of bottles in the wagon with them and they had been nipping at them. But there was also a fair quantity of hot chocolate ingested perhaps less than an hour prior to their deaths. It's kind of hard to pinpoint time of death exactly because of the weather, but the chocolate seems to have been ingested sometime after the kids began the hay ride, and there was nothing in the wagon contents to indicate that a thermos or other container of chocolate had been available."

Red groaned. "Well, that narrows the field to half a dozen possibilities. Charles and I have been tracing the kids' ride for most of the day. It seems it was not only a hay ride, but a chance for them to go Christmas caroling."

"They stopped at the nursing home where they were given hot chocolate," Charles put in. "Then they stopped at old Mr. Stanley's house with more hot chocolate."

"Then they stopped at Lynn Christman's," Red continued, "and the Jacobs and Hein place and even that principal's place."

"All served hot chocolate?" Harden said, unbelieving.

"Yep, and cookies, and cupcakes, and apples, and God only knows what else," Red said.

"Hein and Jacobs said the kids didn't go in to their place," Charles corrected. "No goodies there."

Harden scratched his chin and raised an eyebrow. "Well, that explains all the junk food in their systems. Guess they all didn't eat all they were offered," he said. "Singer mentioned that there was a plastic bag in with the box of folded clothes. It had some apples and cookies in it. I just thought it was something the kids took along on the ride. He said they would test the food for any drugs." Harden shuffled through a stack of papers on his desk and then looked up. "What do you think about Will Lester's performance?"

Red shook his head. "What do you know about the guy?" he asked.

"Not much," Hardin admitted. "I've seen him around for some time now. He seemed pretty quiet and level headed until the stunt he pulled last night."

"He's on parole," Red offered. "He got mixed up with a pretty rough bunch in Mandan where he grew up. He was arrested for rape and assault with a deadly weapon a few years ago."

Dr. Hardin raised his eyebrows and looked genuinely shocked. "How did he get here then?"

"He had been put on the work release program and did some road work for a while. Then Easter agreed to hire him on the farm. There's a stipulation that he can't go back to the Mandan area while he's on parole. I think the family of the girl would like nothing better than to see him back in jail."

"You don't think . . ." Hardin asked, leaving the sentence to trail off.

"Well," Whitedeer said, "it seems he had a fight with Mr. Easter Friday morning. That's why he was out. Easter said he suspected that Will took his girl to the plane in Bismarck by the miles accumulated on the vehicle he was driving. Then Will admitted it to us as well."

"Could he have been mad enough to pull something like that?" Hardin wondered.

"Don't know," Red said, "but I sure as hell plan to find out. The State boys took latent fingerprints from everything they could."

"Of course," Hardin interposed, "considering what he did with the clothes, bodies and all, his fingerprints are going to be every place anyway."

"There's more," Red said and proceeded to tell the doctor about the burning jacket and the questionably matching button. "So Charles brought him back to town and we are holding him as a material witness right now," he concluded.

"Good Lord!" Dr. Hardin said, "if the kid's not guilty he sure as hell did everything in his power to make himself appear to be."

Red sighed and got to his feet. "It would make it almost too easy if that's the case, wouldn't it? But I've got a call in to the Swensons who just happen not to be at home. I'll check with Mavis about the trip to Bismarck and all. I'd hate to believe it was Will but I also find it hard to swallow all his excuses for what he did." He put on his hat and walked out the door behind Whitedeer.

XVII

"So where do we go from here?" the deputy asked as the two men left the hospital and walked to where the sheriff had parked his car. It was already past 5:00 p. m.

"The Bennett place, I guess," Strickland said, getting behind the wheel of the car and starting the motor. "This interview's got to be short because we need to get to the school by 6:00 but at least we'll get a feel for his situation. What do you think of Bennett's chance of being our killer?" He maneuvered the car carefully through the mounting snow drifts.

"Possible, but not probable. He probably has the temper and even perhaps the mentality for something like it, but not the means."

"How so?" Red had worked with his chief deputy for several years and come to trust his opinions in most cases and situations. The two men worked well together and Red knew when he retired that he would encourage Whitedeer to run for the office of sheriff. Bannah could do worse.

"I don't think he drives. It would have been a pretty long walk back to town from where that wagon was stopped, to say nothing of getting to wherever he boarded it, especially as cold as it was, and another thing, if the kids were drugged I can't see them having stopped at his house. There was no love lost between him and them and even given the Christmas spirit and all, it doesn't seem likely."

"He could have had an accomplice," Strickland said, playing Devil's Advocate.

"I don't think there's anyone in town that close to him, unless it would be his mother. Think she is up to whacking people into pieces?"

Strickland dutifully grinned at the attempted levity. The sky had turned completely dark by the time the two men pulled their car into the Bennett's driveway. The house seemed dark from the front, but a thin patch of light shown on the snow of the side yard. The two men walked to what was presumably the kitchen door and knocked.

Mrs. Bennett was a frail, little woman, not quite five feet tall. Her face registered puzzlement and then, Strickland thought, fear as she recognized the two men standing on the doorstep.

"May we come in?" Strickland asked.

Mrs. Bennett stepped back in tacit consent and the two men entered the kitchen. The room was bleak and spare. A wooden table with two chairs sat before the windows. On the opposite wall was a day bed on which a dark man with unshaved face sat. A single sink was wedged behind the kitchen door, an old, wheezing refrigerator and small electric stove made up the rest of the room's contents. The wallpapered walls were peeling and there was not a picture or a plant to brighten up the bleak little room.

"Donald Bennett?" Strickland asked, looking at the man who had not seemed to notice the entry of the two officers. The man looked at Strickland and nodded.

"Can we ask you a few questions?"

"About what?" Mrs. Bennett interrupted.

"I'm sure you heard about what happened last night," Strickland said. The bulk of the two officers filled the small room to overflowing. They had not been offered a seat and so stood uncomfortably in the middle of the room.

"We heard it on the radio this mornin', but Donald didn't have nothin' to do with them!" Mrs. Bennett blurted.

"No one said he did," Strickland assured. "We just want to find out what

Donald knew about the kids involved."

The man met Strickland's eyes. "I didn't like 'em," he said. "I don't like *your daughter,* or *his sister* either," he said, pointing to Charles. But I didn't do anythin' to hurt 'em."

"But you did attack a teacher, is that right?"

Bennett dropped his gaze. "I lost my temper a little," he mumbled.

Mrs. Bennett's face registered shock. "You never told . . ."

Donald Bennett glared at his mother. "It was none of your damn business," he said. "I said I wasn't going back to that damn school and that was all you need to know!"

"Where were you both last night?" Strickland persisted.

"We was right here," Mrs. Bennett said, too quickly. We didn't leave the house all evening."

"Did you see the kids in the hay wagon?"

The woman's face paled and she exchanged a look with her son who stared straight ahead. "No . . ." she said.

"That's funny," Red challenged. "Your neighbors across the way saw them." It was a bluff but one worth trying, he thought.

Again mother and son exchanged looks. "Okay," Donald said grudgingly, not meeting Strickland's eyes. "They drove by here about eleven. They were raising a racket, singin' and laughin.' Mom had just got back from . . ." He shut his mouth abruptly, realizing what he had said.

"I thought the two of you were here all evening," Red pounced.

Mrs. Bennett raised her hands and then dropped them back into her lap. "I'd gone to church, prayer meetin', you know. It was longer than usual."

"Are you sure of the time the kids came by?" Red continued.

"Yes," Mrs. Bennett said. "I got home before eleven and we hadn't gone to bed when we heard them kids makin' noise."

"Is this the story the two of you plan to stick with now?" Red asked.

Donald sprang to his feet, fists clenched, and advanced toward his mother. "You never keep your damn mouth shut!" He looked angry enough to strike her. The little woman shrank back in the chair.

Red and Charles both jumped forward and, grabbing the man by the shoulders, forced him back to his seat. "I'm going to be checking up on you," Red said, angrily glaring at the man who met his gaze defiantly. "If I find you ever lay a hand on your mother--or anyone else, for that matter-- you are going to be a long-term guest in my jail! Got that?"

Donald dropped his gaze at last and nodded.

Strickland continued, "if you should think of anything that might help us, let us know."

"We don't get or make no phone calls," Donald Bennett said, sulking, "We won't think of nothin' neither!" He glowered in anger but whether at the officers, his mother or life in general, they couldn't say.

As Strickland and Whitedeer turned to leave, Charles asked, almost as if an afterthought, "Hey, Donald, do you own a brown jacket or coat?"

Again mother and son exchanged glances. "I do," Mrs. Bennett admitted. "I wore it last night."

"May we see it?" Strickland asked.

"You ain't got no warrant," Donald said, again standing to his feet.

Mrs. Bennett, uncharacteristically firm, pushed her son back onto the day bed. "It don't matter, Donny," she said. "I got nothin' to hide." With that she went into the next room and returned with a tan corduroy car coat with all buttons intact.

"Thank you for your co-operation, Mrs. Bennett," Red said as he returned her coat. The two men again moved toward the door. "We will keep in touch just in case either of you should think of anything else." They left the little room and got back into their car. The snow had begun falling more heavily now and the wind once again was picking up.

"Hard to believe it's snowed this whole day," Whitedeer said. "Scratch anything being left at the murder scene now for sure."

"I don't think the Bennetts had anything to do with the killings, but they are trying to hide something," Strickland said almost to himself. Then he looked toward the deputy. "Better call in and see if there is anything else. Otherwise I am ready to head for the school."

The deputy made the radio call and, finding that the dispatcher had nothing new for them, hung the microphone back in place on the dash board. "I think his mom's scared of him," he said, "Bennett's mom." He clarified although Strickland knew who he meant.

XVIII

By the time the two men pulled up in front of the school house it was well past 6 p.m. The sky which had been dropping snow for nearly the entire day had now cleared and a big silver moon hung low in the east. Charles pointed to the Chevy Blazer parked near the school entrance. "I see Paula's here," he observed. The parking lot was almost completely filled with cars and there were knots of people standing just outside the double doors that led into the building. There were mounds of offerings sitting just outside the door: flowers already wilting from the cold, teddy bears, envelopes, cards, the mute offerings of people who grieve and need to show it. Charles looked at Red and mutely shook his head. "I guess I should have figured the parents would be here too."

"I hadn't really thought about it but it's to be expected. These people need to hear what's happening from us and not just from the rumors flying all over town."

The two men approached the group of people and were surprised when they parted silently and allowed their entrance into the building without comment and then silently followed them in. They were also surprised as they entered the study hall to note how quiet everyone was. The students had grouped themselves at the back of the room while the teachers and other staff members had gathered at the front. Then it seemed that their entrance was a signal for everyone to begin talking at once. " What happened…understand . . . friends…good students . . ." It was a blur of voices, words, sounds.

The two men moved to the front of the room and Strickland held up his hand for silence. He met Penny's gaze and smiled slightly. She and Paula had placed themselves a little apart from the rest of the group. "I'll try not to keep any of you too long and I'll try to make this as painless as possible," Red began. "I want you all to think of anything that might have happened in the last few days, something as trivial as an argument between any of you and your dead classmates. I want to know if you've seen any strangers around, anything that looked suspicious or unusual. If you can think of anything, even if you think it is something unimportant or stupid, now or in the future, please call me at home or the sheriff's department. If for some reason you can't find me, Chief Deputy Whitedeer here will be happy to take your information. The important thing is report any and everything." Red put his hand on the deputy's shoulder, as if all did not already know who he was.

The students sat silently but exchanging looks with one another. A tall, blond boy raised his hand. " There was this car," he began. "It's kind of old and beat up, a Ford I think, but it's been cruising around the neighborhood and around the parking lot for the last few days. It's . . . um . . . kind of a dirty green with a dented right front fender."

"Oh, that's just my dumb uncle, Billy Joe," a short dark-haired girl in glasses spoke up. "He's here for the holidays and he's been dropping me off and picking me up."

"Who are you?" Red asked.

"I'm Natalie Blair," the girl said. "My dad works at the new power plant and my mom's secretary at the power company."

"Where does your uncle live?" Charles asked.

"With us," the girl said, and the students burst into restrained laughter.

"I mean when he's not visiting here," Charles said, trying to hide his own smile.

"Oh, he's from South Carolina," Natalie said. "He's never seen snow and never been in a cold climate before."

"Is he outside waiting for you now?" Red asked. "Why don't you go out and call him in?"

The girl shook her head. "No, my mom brought me this evening and dropped me off but you can come see Uncle Billy Joe at our house."

Red made a note of the girl's address and then looked around the room again. "Anything else?" he asked.

"Mr. Schmidt was yelling at Ted and Brad something fierce the other afternoon," a short pudgy boy at the back of the room offered.

Strickland and Whitedeer both turned their eyes to the basketball coach who was standing in the corner of the room looking out the window. "Is that true, Conrad?" Strickland asked.

The coach turned his attention back to the room. "Yes it is," he admitted. "I caught both of them smoking after practice and they know that breaks their training. I told both of them if I caught them again they'd be off the team for the rest of the year."

Red nodded and the man went back to his contemplation of the outside world.

"I don't believe this really had anything to do with the students or faculty," William Hein said. "It's simply too unthinkable to believe that anyone in this school or in this town for that matter could commit such a terrible crime."

Lynn Christman, who had been sitting directly in front of where Red was standing, nodded in agreement. "I, too, cannot believe these killings were the product of anyone presently in this room or in this town for that matter."

Red exchanged a long look with his deputy and then decided to drop his bombshell. "Oh yes," he said, "it was definitely not only someone in this town but someone who knew these kids very well. Several of you admit to having had the kids stop in and having given the kids hot chocolate. Well, one of their visits got them enough drugs to put an elephant to sleep. Now I just want to know where all they were and who all was passing out goodies."

Lynn Christman's face blanched and she put her head down on the desk. "Oh my God!" she moaned. "I can't believe this. It's too awful!"

The silence in the room was then complete. The clock hanging at the front of the study hall could be heard through the whole room. In a minute or two people once again turned to their neighbors and began shocked commentary.

"So now you see why it's so important that we learn anything and everything that has transpired in the last few days." Red Strickland said, raising his hand to still the conversations.

"Miss Christman made Penny and James do extra work because they were passing notes," Betsy Klein said, and turned a vindictive gaze toward Penny, whose face reddened.

"I don't consider discipline for bad school behavior to be a reason sufficient for murder," Red said. "Now tell me, Betsy, do you?"

The girl hung her head and said nothing.

When it became clear that there was going to be no additional revelations forthcoming, Red told the people that was all he had for the evening and they could leave unless there were further questions or comments. "Remember, please, anything you think of that might shed some light on this matter . . . whether you are still in town or have gone for your vacation . . . please let us know."

Again it was eerily quiet as students, parents and finally teachers began filing from the room. Red sensed the underlying hostility of some of the parents. Now that it was known for certain that someone they all knew and trusted had been responsible for this outrage he feared for what might happen in the days to come.

The two men were the last to leave the school room. "We better find out something soon," Charles said in a whisper. "This doesn't feel good." Strickland nodded.

"Enough drugs to kill an elephant?" the deputy continued softly as they made their way down the quiet hallway. "We aren't even sure yet that they were really drugged."

Strickland turned to face his deputy. "I'm sure of it," he said. "That answers so many of the things we were wondering about at the murder scene, like how the six of them could all be subdued by what I'm now sure was only one person." As they stepped outside, they turned up the collars of their coats. Once again the sky had clouded over and the snow had begun to fall heavily.

SUNDAY

Late Sunday morning the snow had finally stopped, the sky was blue and the air was extremely cold. Penny woke to the sonorous tolling of church bells calling the various Bannah congregations to morning worship. She rubbed her eyes sleepily and for just a minute felt a feeling of warmth and peace. Then she remembered her friends and the events of the past twenty-four hours. She angrily threw back the covers and carefully swung her legs off the side of the bed. Boots gave a meow of protest as he crawled from under the blanket she had carelessly allowed to cover him up. Penny smiled and absent mindedly scratched the cat under the chin. After belting her fleecy robe around her and slipping on green, fuzzy slippers, she made slow progress to the bathroom. Fifteen minutes later she entered the kitchen, where her father was dishing up generous bowls of hot oatmeal to which he had added lavish amounts of brown sugar and raisins.

"I'll sure be glad to get rid of this cast," Penny grumbled as she slid onto her chair. "Those sponge baths don't really leave me feeling clean."

Nodding sympathetically, her father set her bowl of oatmeal in front of her. "The toast is almost ready too, Hon," he said. "Dig in. Want some juice, milk or coffee?"

"All three, I think today, thank you." Penny carefully spooned some of her oatmeal into a saucer and added a bit of cream. She leaned over and slid the dish under her chair.

"You spoil that cat," Red laughed as Boots settled down to his Sunday treat.

"Guess it's too late to change my ways now, or his either." Penny laughed and accepted a slice of buttered toast from her father.

Just as Red began his own breakfast, the phone rang shrilly. Making a face, he rose to answer it. A few minutes later he sat back down at the table, frowning.

"Something about the murders?" Penny inquired.

"That was the state crime lab," Red said. "They got back with the evaluation of the hot chocolate your friends had been given. There was enough Trazodone and Valium in that chocolate to have put an elephant to sleep." He smiled to himself, remembering his exchange with his deputy the previous evening.

Penny sighed. "Then at least maybe they didn't know what was happening," she said.

"Also something very strange," Red went on musingly. "The boot print we cast has fibers in it. The guys are going to do more testing to see if they can come up with just what it is. And I guess Will Lester can go home too," Red continued. "The material on the button and on the remains of his jacket isn't the same material according to the lab."

"I'm glad," Penny said. "I only met him a few times when we were having a party out at Jim's place, but he seemed nice enough."

"I'm glad too," Red admitted, "but it does leave us right back where we started." He left the table, nibbling a piece of toast in his hand, and went to the phone where he called his office and instructed the deputy on duty to release Will Lester and drive him home, if necessary. Then he returned to his breakfast, buttering a second piece of toast.

"What about Donald Bennett? Did you talk to him?" Penny asked, mumbling through the bite of oatmeal she had just spooned into her mouth.

"We checked him out. He's strange alright but I don't believe he did it."

II

Whitedeer was already seated at his desk in the office when the Sheriff walked in. "You're here early," Red commented, pitching his hat as usual onto the corner of his own desk.

"I wanted to look over the stuff we got from the interviews yesterday. I don't think there's much chance of finding anyone at home until church is out," Charles added. "Lots of people who probably have not darkened a church door for years will be there today, just because of the shock of what's happened."

"You're probably right," Red agreed. He pulled up a chair and proceeded to tell his deputy of the laboratory findings on the stomach contents of the victims as well as the news about Will Lester. "Anything from those reporters this morning?" he asked, settling himself with a cup of coffee.

"That redhead called earlier, to answer your question," Charles said. "She says we're being uncooperative."

"Damned sensation seekers," Red muttered, "I suppose they've been out bothering the families as well."

"You know it."

"Any problem with releasing Lester?"

"Nope, I told him that we will want to talk to him again and not to leave town without telling us. Then Joe gave him a ride back to the farm." With that the deputy turned back to the pile of papers on the desk and Red went into his own office to begin another day.

III

Betsy Klein had a problem. She thoughtfully chewed on her pencil eraser as she waited for a customer to check out at the Movieland VCR rental store where she worked part time. She liked the extra money her job got her, but when her parents found out what her grades for this semester would be, giving up her job would be the least of her problems. She knew she had done poorly on almost every exam she had taken the week prior to the holidays. Now what was there to do about it? She got to her feet and went to the index cards which showed the paid-up customers and a record of their movie rentals. When she found the cards she was looking for, she read the list of movies rented, and a smile of satisfaction played over her plump features.

It was only an idea, a dumb idea, and if it didn't work, well, then it didn't work. But she thought it might be worth a try. She didn't really think any of those people had a connection with the gruesome happenings on Friday night, but if any of them had, perhaps her parents would never need to know how poorly she had been doing this semester. The problem was Betsy didn't exactly know how to go about doing what she wanted to. She was an avid reader of detective and mystery stories, and that, as a matter of fact, writing them was what she really wanted to do when she got out of high school. She wanted to be a writer; so, what would a character in one of her stories do given the same opportunity? Mulling over her problem and what to do about it, she continued the rather easy job of renting movies to the few customers who came in.

At 6:00 p.m., Helen Sanders, the owner of Movieland, came in to relieve her and finish out the day until the 8:00 p.m. closing.

Betsy walked home, crunching snow beneath her boots as she made her plans. She would have to wait until her parents were not home to carry them out. Fortunately, her mother and father spent most Sunday evenings playing bridge with the neighbors. The only difficulty was that some weeks it was done in the Klein home. She entered the front door and hurried into the kitchen to find her mother removing a casserole from the oven. "Please set the table, Betsy," her mother said. "We want to be at the Fosters before seven." That solved part of the problem!

Betsy ran to her room and dumped the movie tapes she had brought home on her bed. She wanted to see some of them in the privacy of her own room on her own VCR. She dumped her coat and scarf there as well and slipped off her boots and left them in the corner. She would straighten up everything later. The most important thing was to get her parents on their way! She hurried back to the kitchen and dutifully helped her mother finish the dinner.

"You seem in a more cheerful mood than you've been in for the past few days," her father observed as they were finishing dinner.

"I feel so bad about the kids," Betsy said, cramming a huge bite of chocolate cake into her mouth. "I wonder when the funerals will be."

"Tuesday, from what I hear," Betsy's father said. "I think they are going to have a single service at the high school auditorium."

Betsy's mother got up from the table and began clearing away the leftovers. "You don't mind loading the dishwasher for me, do you, Dear," she asked over her shoulder. "I really do need to get ready."

Betsy was so relieved to have her parents out of the house that she offered no objections to the usually dreary task of after-dinner cleanup. When her parents were safely out of the house and the dishwasher was rumbling in the kitchen, Betsy returned to her room and inserted the first of the movies into her VCR. An hour later, after sampling bits of each of the movies she had smuggled home, Betsy was a little surer of her ground. It was still something that was almost impossible to contemplate, but after all, she could at least try the bait. If the persons didn't want some of their little secrets out, well, then she would have a lovely second semester.

Wanting to be certain that she would not be overheard and that her parents might not unexpectedly have come home, Betsy decided to make her calls from the kitchen telephone. She pulled up a stool and wrote several phone numbers from the directory on a sheet she tore from the telephone note pad. Then she dialed each of the numbers she had written in turn. To each person who answered, Betsy made the same statement: "I know something about you," Betsy intoned in a hoarse whisper which she hoped would adequately disguise her normally shrill voice. "If you don't want the sheriff to know about the movies you like to watch, I have a deal." Each time there was stunned silence from the other end of the line. "I want to make a deal," Betsy repeated into the phone.

Silence, then, "What are you talking about?"

"The kids on the hay ride," Betsy whispered. "You know what happened to them and I think you made it happen."

The reactions to each of her calls varied slightly, but were usually "Who is this and what do you want?" or "I don't know what you are talking about!" followed by the click of the phone and a dial tone.

After her last call, Betsy smiled grimly. She was certain that among the people she had called, she had talked to the killer. Now she didn't know if she dared follow through with any demands. She certainly didn't want to end up like those stupid kids had. Then she had an idea. Supposing she wrote a pretend story. She would get input as to what she should do as the story's heroine. After all, she would just be wanting advice about a story.

One of the persons Betsy had called smiled grimly as he replaced the phone receiver gently back in its cradle. He had been around too long not to know a thing or two. She thought she had disguised her voice well, but he was sure he knew who the caller had been. If the game was up, he would have to do some massive housecleaning.

MONDAY

Mrs. Cooley let herself into the Strickland house at precisely 7:00 a. m. She was gratified that both the Stricklands were still apparently asleep. She made her way quietly to the kitchen and made coffee. Then she busied herself with the breakfast preparation.

A few minutes later Red Strickland greeted her with a pleasant "Good morning." He walked over to the table and sat down.

Mrs. Cooley clicked her tongue sympathetically. "Terrible thing that happened this past weekend," she observed, filling a mug with coffee and setting it in front of the sheriff.

"Yes," he agreed. "I'm afraid it's going to be a hard one to solve, especially now that we know it isn't a stranger."

Mrs. Cooley nodded, then glanced at the doorway where Penny stood leaning on her crutch. "I know you can't tell me what you know," she said, "but I've known most of these people for most of my life and I can't believe it's someone who's lived here longer than two or three years."

"I almost hate to ask this," Strickland said, turning to face the housekeeper. "Did the kids happen to come by your place Friday evening?"

Mrs. Cooley smiled in sad remembrance. "If you mean did they stop in, the answer is no. If you mean did they come by, making enough noise to rattle our windows, then the answer is yes."

"Do you remember about what time?" Red asked.

"It must have been near midnight," Sarah answered. "Carl and I had been in bed for quite some time when we heard the kids laughing and singing and making quite a racket."

Penny left the doorway and kissed her father as she passed his chair on the way to her own. She dug in the pocket of her robe and pulled out a wad of tissues and dabbed at her eyes. "Oh, Mrs. Cooley," she said, not even trying to hide the tears that spilled over and ran down her cheeks. "I can't believe … er … they were so happy and now they're just … *gone!*"

The housekeeper put her arms around the girl's shaking shoulders and patted her cheek. "And there's nothing I can say that will make things any better, Honey," she soothed.

Penny pulled herself to her feet and walked to the sink where she ran cold water and splashed it on her hot cheeks. She turned to face the two people who meant the most in the world to her and suddenly began to shake.

Strickland leaped from his chair and gathered her into his arms. "What is it, Kitten?" he whispered, holding her in his arms and smoothing her hair back off her face. "Why don't you just go back to bed for awhile."

Penny shook her head and finally pulled herself away from her father. "It's only now hit me, Daddy," she whispered. *"I could have been with them!"*

Red took his daughter back to her chair and carefully seated her, arranging her napkin on her lap. "I've been thinking about that all weekend," he admitted, resuming his own seat.

The three sat in silence for awhile, each wrapped in feelings of sorrow, anger and guilt. Boots, sensing the drama unfolding around him, and not wanting to be left out, suddenly gave out a loud meow of protest. After all, his stomach was being badly neglected!

Penny looked at her father and tried a shaky smile. "Dr. Harden promised a walking cast today, Daddy," she said. Boots leaped up into her lap before she could settle her chair nearer the table. Penny rubbed her face against the cat's soft fur. "Hasn't anyone fed you yet, Poor Baby," she crooned to the now purring cat.

"As if anyone could enter this kitchen without feeding that cat," Mrs. Cooley said, entering the spirit of trying to lighten Penny's obvious misery. "What would you like for breakfast, Dear?"

"Bacon and eggs and pancakes and fresh-squeezed orange juice since I'm not the one who has to fix it," Penny suggested, as she dumped Boots gently on to the floor.

Mrs. Cooley smiled at her. "Would you settle for just the bacon and eggs and orange juice?"

"Well, if I must, I must," Penny agreed. "Can't get away with anything around here!"

"Just wait until you get out of that cast, young lady," her father said, accepting his plate from Mrs. Cooley. "You can start pulling your share of the work around here."

"Now don't be hard on the girl," the housekeeper chided. "She's always been a big help to me without being asked." She smiled as she said it.

"Glad to hear she's worth something." Red grinned, and broke off a bit of bacon from his plate, dropping it to the very interested cat who was now seated beside his chair.

After breakfast, Red waited for Penny to get dressed and bundled into her coat and scarf. "I'll drop you at Doc's office for your cast, and I guess you should call Mrs. Cooley to pick you up after you are done."

"That's okay, Daddy," Penny said, carefully walking down the steps and crossing to the driveway. "Paula has said she would pick me up this morning. We want to go to the library and get some books."

"For those extra reports you got piled on you?" Red said looking sternly at his daughter.

"Oh, Daddy," Penny objected. "I would have told you before the new term started. I sure didn't need Betsy Klein shooting her mouth off!"

Red opened the car door and helped her in. "Be sure your sins will find you out, Daughter!" he said mockingly, with a deep, gruff voice and a twinkle in his eye.

II

Red delivered his daughter to the doctor's office, then drove to his own. He wondered where he should go now in his investigation. Many of the teachers had left for their own holiday vacations, and there seemed to be so little to go on. Perhaps the state crime lab had come up with something more from all the materials they had taken for examination.

Whitedeer greeted him as he entered the office. "Want to go to the drug store with me?" Strickland said, not bothering to remove his coat. "We can check the records for those Trazodone and Valium prescriptions."

"Sure," Whitedeer said, getting his own coat and hat. "I'll bet you half the people in Bannah are on some kind of pills for sleep or depression. Don't count on that helping much."

"That and that button are the only concrete leads we have to go on," Strickland grumbled. "Let's walk to the drug store, Charles, I think the cold air might clear my mind."

Len Jacobs greeted the two men when they entered the door. "How can I be of help?"

"We need to see your prescription records," Strickland said.

"I don't know if I can do that legally without my patrons' permission," Jacobs objected. He stood with his thick, muscular arms crossed over his chest, his square jaw jutting out like a fighter about to leave his corner.

"You can show us the records we need now, or I can go to Judge Mercer and get a warrant; just bear in mind it's time we can hardly afford to waste," the sheriff observed.

"Okay," Jacobs said, dropping his hands and turning away from them. "If it's something to do with the murders, you can come back to my office. It's kind of crowded and cluttered, but you can have a little peace and quiet in there anyway."

An hour later the two men emerged from the pharmacist's office. "Any help?" Jacobs asked from the counter were he was sacking several prescriptions.

"It's still hard to tell," Strickland said. "Thanks for your co-operation, anyway."

"Glad to help," Jacobs said. "I've been racking my brains ever since Charles stopped at our house Saturday," he went on. "I just can't believe it was anyone in this town who could have committed such a terrible crime."

The two officers had left the drugstore and were about to return to the office when they were accosted by John Stover, owner and editor of the town newspaper, *The Bannah Star*. "Hey, Sheriff," he said, deliberately planting his huge frame on the sidewalk in front of the two men. "If I didn't know better I'd think you were avoiding the press."

"What makes you think you know better?" Strickland scowled and attempted to make his way around the still figure.

"Come on, Red," Stover grinned, "I've got to make a living too."

"I suppose so," Strickland agreed, "Unfortunately there's nothing I can tell you."

"Well, you could begin with just what it was you found at the Easter farm Saturday morning."

"I could, but I won't," Red said, this time managing to sidestep Stover's bulk. "When there is news worth printing, I'll be the first to tell you. Otherwise, if you're looking for sensationalism, you are going to have to find it somewhere else."

"You're interfering with the public's right to know," Stover grumbled, following after the two men. "Wouldn't it be better to tell the people the truth in my newspaper rather than let them continue with all their gruesome speculations?"

Strickland turned to face the irate newspaper man. "Look," he growled, "I'm going to tell you just what I've been telling the other news hounds. When I have something to report I'll call a news conference. Until then there is no news!"

"The fact this damned thing happened in the first place was bad enough," Whitedeer said as the two men continued down Main Street. "What does he want, a blow-by-blow description?"

III

"Call Bismarck," Millie called out as the two men had barely gotten into the sheriff's office. "Crime Lab has something for you." Whitedeer sat on the corner of the sheriff's desk as the sheriff put in his call.

"Strickland here at Bannah," Red began. "Someone has something for me?" As he listened to the caller, he pulled a yellow pad to him, picked up a pencil and began jotting notes. When he hung up the phone, he scowled. "I had hoped there might be a break here, but I'm not sure."

"What?" Millie and Charles asked together.

"There were some minute blood stains found on the back of that button," Strickland confided. "The blood appears to be O-Negative, so could be from some of the kids, or the killer."

"I wonder if they will ever really be able to perfect getting a person's DNA," Charles mused. "It would sure make a cop's job a lot easier."

Red continued, "They said the button doesn't appear to have been pulled off the coat, it just fell off, no threads clinging or any thing like that. I would have thought if the button had come from the coat the killer was wearing, there would be quite a bit of evidence of blood staining; unless, of course, the button had fallen off before the killings began."

"Sounds like maybe Miss Christman might have had the right idea that the killer had two coats," Charles said. "Maybe we do need to contact the cleaners."

"Also," Strickland said, now doodling on the pad before him. "The fibers off that shoe cast appear to be wool. Might either be something picked up from the carpet in the killer's home . . . or . . ." he stopped doodling and drew something he then held up for Charles to see.

"A stocking?" Charles queried. "A sock? But how would a sock get there?"

"It might be a crazy idea," Strickland said, "but how about the killer putting socks over his boots? It would diminish if not totally obliterate the pattern of the boot."

"So now on top of everything else we've got to locate a pair of wool socks?" Charles ran his hand through his hair in frustration. "Should be easy, can't be more than seven or eight thousand of those in drawers around town."

"You can try the cleaners now if you want to," Strickland said. "Somehow I think the killer might be too smart to have the damage repaired in a public place. Usually coats and jackets have an extra button somewhere. The killer will probably do his own repair work."

"He's got to slip up somewhere," Whitedeer grumbled as he headed for the door. "If there was a little blood on the button, maybe there's just a little blood on the coat too."

"So do you check every closet in Bannah?" Millie asked, looking up from her typewriter.

Red grimaced. "If we have to, we have to," he observed dryly.

IV

Penny felt somewhat better with her walking cast. The doctor had also exchanged the crutch for a cane. "Just until you get used to the new cast," He had said. Now she and Paula had entered the public library and checked out the books they had needed for their respective history reports. Mr. Hein had told them these reports would be needed at the end of the first six weeks in the second semester. Both girls had previously agreed that getting the research and writing of the reports out now during Christmas vacation would allow them time for more interesting things when the school term, and especially the basketball season, were again in full swing. Talking about this as they drove from the library reminded both the girls of the three dead boys and the fact that they would now not be on the basketball team.

"I never thought I would consider a broken leg to be a lucky thing," Penny confided, "but if it hadn't been for that leg, at least one more of us would be dead."

Paula shuddered at the thought. She was a dark-haired, dark-eyed girl, tall for her age, and such a contrast to Penny's pert blondness and bubbly nature. Yet the two girls, for the most part, had become good friends, especially since the beginning of their senior year. Penny and Paula had both decided on Jamestown College for their future schooling. Now as they drove from the library, the two girls decided to stop in at the café for a Coke.

Molly Jackson, the morning waitress, came to their booth with menus and glasses of water, a smile on her face.

"Nothing to eat, Mrs. Jackson," Penny said, beginning to return the menu. "Oh, or did you want something, Paula?"

The other girl shook her head and returned her menu as well. "Just a Coke for me," she said.

"I think I'll have a cup of hot chocolate," Penny said. She became quiet but there was a soft look in her eyes and a smile on her lips.

"Why the smile?" Paula asked.

"I was thinking of the first day Tracy Wilkins came to school," Penny replied. "Mrs. Kramer stood her up in front of the class and told her to introduce herself and tell us something about herself."

"When was that?" Paula asked.

"Third grade," Penny said. "Tracy was such a little thing, smaller than the rest of us for sure. She stood there for a couple minutes then put her little fists on her hips and said, 'My name is Tracy Wilkins, my mom and dad are dead and I don't like you and I don't want to be here!'"

Paula laughed. "She always seemed so quiet and shy to me," she said. "That took a lot of nerve."

Penny reached up to brush away the tear that slid down her face. "I liked her from that first minute. I admired her spunk . . . and now . . ."

Paula looked across Penny's shoulder, out the front window. "Don't look now, but here comes *Mr. Turtle,*" she said.

The high school principal saw Paula looking at him through the glass, waved and turned to enter the café. "That spoils the morning," Paula mumbled as Sam Tuttle approached their table.

"No crutch, Penny," he noted, pausing beside their booth.

"No, sir," Penny said, "just the cane and walking cast for awhile longer, the doctor said. But it was sure good to scratch!"

"Coffee, Sam?" Molly called from behind the counter. The two girls exchanged a glance. It seemed odd to hear the principal addressed by his first name.

"That's fine, Molly," Tuttle said, taking a seat in the booth directly behind them.

"That must be a new coat," Paula whispered, leaning across the booth.

"He looks even more like a turtle in it," Penny hid her smile behind her hand. Tuttle had on a navy blue down-filled jacket which did, indeed, almost obscure his short neck.

"Terrible thing about your classmates," he said, when their drinks had been set before them, and Molly had left to get his change. The two girls nodded. "I don't suppose your dad has any leads, does he, Penny?"

"Only a . . ." Penny began, and then clamped her lips closed tightly. Just in time she had remembered her father admonishing her not to mention either the button or the drugged chocolate to anyone!

"Yes, go on," Tuttle urged.

"Oh nothing, I was just going to say . . . er," her mind raced frantically for something plausible, "the place where the . . . the . . . thing happened."

Tuttle's eyebrows raised slightly. "Oh," he said, "I hadn't realized they had found the murder scene."

Penny looked at Paula helplessly. She felt she had only gotten in deeper than she had been before. She wondered if that was part of the secret too.

"They found it. It didn't help," Paula added now. "It started to snow heavily right after they found the place, my brother said, they could not find much there."

"Too bad," Tuttle said, quickly finishing his coffee. A minute later he left the café, leaving the two girls to look at one another.

"I sure hope Dad didn't mean that to be a secret too," Penny confided.

Paula leaned across the table. "Do you know more?"

"What has Charles told you?"

"Not much," Paula said. "He said I should keep an eye open for people wearing, or maybe not wearing, brown corduroy coats or jackets."

"They found a button," Penny whispered. "Please don't tell anyone. I don't think Daddy would mind us talking about it to each other. After all, your brother knows everything Daddy knows."

The two girls finished their drinks, left a small tip for the waitress and walked out the front door and down the sidewalk, Penny using her cane to test for icy spots as they walked. "Oh, I knew about that and the drugs," Paula said. "It gives me the shivers to think that something like that could have been planned."

"The whole thing gives me the shivers," Penny admitted. "I've racked my brain to try and think of anyone in this town who could even think of doing such a thing."

"Well, you know," Paula said, "they say poison is a woman's weapon. You don't suppose . . ."

"Good God!" Penny blurted, trying to suppress a shudder, "it's hard enough thinking that a man could kill our friends, but a woman . . . no way! And we're not just looking at the drugs," she reminded her friend, "but what was done afterwards! No way! It just couldn't be a woman!"

"I'm sure you're right," Paula agreed, climbing up a snow drift and sliding down the other side. She walked around and unlocked the car doors. "Sure glad the storekeepers at least are so good to keep the sidewalks shoveled."

Penny eased herself into the passenger side of the Blazer by balancing herself on her cane and swinging her good leg onto the step. "The drifts have gotten so high from the snow plows on the streets it's nearly impossible to park anywhere," she observed. "Mrs. Jackson's son, Paul, you know the little boy with all those freckles, has been shoveling out our driveway this winter. I'm sure once I'm totally out of this cast Daddy will decide it's good exercise for me."

Paula laughed as she slammed the driver's door. "You're lucky you don't live nearly out in the country like we do," she observed. "I've already earned my share of exercise and winter has barely started."

The two girls were silent the rest of the short drive to Penny's house. "Come in for a while," Penny invited, as Paula pulled her car into the Strickland driveway. "I can give you that book you need for your report."

Paula and Penny entered the kitchen. "Something sure smells good," Paula said.

Mrs. Cooley turned from the oven from where she had just lifted a pan of cinnamon rolls. "I suppose I know two girls who are hungry?"

"Well, as a matter of fact," Penny said, "as good as those rolls smell I know I, for one, am nearly starved."

"Let them cool a bit and you can see how they turned out." Mrs. Cooley placed the pan on a rack. "I'll call you when they are ready."

The two girls went up the stairs and entered Penny's room where Paula dropped onto Penny's bed. "Better not let Mrs. Cooley see you sitting there," Penny warned. "She's hell on wheels when it comes to sitting on beds. She says it breaks down the springs or something."

"I'm not that heavy!" Paula protested.

Penny lay across the end of the bed with her chin in her cupped hands. "Didn't Mr. Tuttle used to wear a brown corduroy coat?"

"Beats me."

"I can't be sure, but ... "

"You're just wanting it to be him."

"How can you think that?"

"Well, he's not the best-liked person in Bannah."

Penny sighed. "I don't want it to be anyone we know," she said. "I think it would be too hard to live with the knowledge that someone you had known all your life, maybe even someone who lived next door, could do something like that."

Paula got up from the bed and went to Penny's bookcase. "You've got so many books. Where's *To Kill a Mockingbird*?"

"Bottom shelf, I think. It's a red covered book."

"Damn that Betsy Klein anyway," Paula grumbled, as she found and pulled the book from its place on the shelf. "I guess I'd better get home and start reading."

"I could give you an outline, but I really think you'll like it if you haven't read it before."

"I'll just read it and suffer. What books are you going to use?"

"God," Penny groaned, "I haven't even given it any thought. I guess I still need three reports, don't I? It's hard to think of going back to school and going on just as though nothing has happened!"

Paula thumbed absently through the book as she resumed her seat on Penny's bed. "I don't think any of us will really fully take it in until we're back and see their empty desks." She passed her sleeve over her face to hide the tears that were brimming in her eyes.

The two girls left Penny's room and returned to the kitchen at Mrs. Cooley's call up the stairs. There they had milk and one of Mrs. Cooley's warm cinnamon rolls and exchanged small talk with the older woman until Paula took her leave, saying she had to be home before her brother.

Penny got up from the table and taking a plate from the cupboard placed four of the rolls on it. After wrapping it with foil, she handed the plate to Paula. "Two for supper and two for breakfast," she said, smiling at the surprised look on Paula's face. "If Charles is anything like Daddy, you'll be lucky to even get one of these."

Sarah smiled to herself, watching the girls. It was good to see the both of them enjoying one another's company.

That evening, after the Stricklands had finished their dinner of Mrs. Cooley's vegetable soup, Penny filled a large Tupperware container with the leftover soup and then laid out several of Mrs. Cooley's cinnamon rolls on a plate.

"What's that for, Kiddo?" Red asked, settling himself with the newspaper.

"You're going to take this food over to Mrs. Nye," Penny said, moving to the hall closet and pulling out his coat and hat.

Red raised a quizzical eyebrow. "What?" he said, refolding the paper and placing it on the table beside his chair.

Penny smiled and met her father's gaze. "I don't think Mrs. Nye probably feels much like cooking," she said, bundling the container of soup and rolls into a bag.

"Will you come with me?"

Penny shook her head. "No, Daddy, I think Mrs. Nye needs you!"

He got up and put on his coat and hat and then gave his daughter a hard hug. "Sometimes you amaze me," he said, kissing her cheek.

The corners of Penny's mouth turned up in a small grin. "You know, Daddy," she said, walking him to the door, "I kind of thought you and Mrs. Nye might make a nice couple, and now . . . well, I'm just sorry I didn't get the chance maybe to have Marcia for a sister."

When he pulled up in front of the Nye house, Red was surprised to find it completely dark. Maybe she's not at home, he thought, getting out of the car and striding up to the porch. Maybe she's even gone to bed. But having come this far, he rang the doorbell and waited.

In a minute a lamp came on in the Nye living room and shortly after that Kathryn Nye came to the door.

Her appearance was shocking. It had only been two days since he had visited her but in that time she had seemed to shrink into herself. Her hair was limp and dull, and her face red and swollen from crying.

"Penny thought you'd like some of Mrs. Cooley's soup and cinnamon rolls," he said, walking past her and heading toward the kitchen. "I'll just put these on the counter and . . ."

She followed him in and when he turned from placing the bag on the counter, she threw herself into his arms. He gently kissed her cheek but she turned her head and found his mouth with hers. She had wrapped her arms around his neck and now pulled his head down fiercely to meet her kiss.

"Please, Red," she whispered. "Make me feel ... make me feel something, *anything!*"

He tried gently to disentangle her arms but her grip was almost strangling him. *"I need to know I'm still alive!"* she sobbed and unbuttoned his coat and pulled it from his shoulders, letting it drop to the floor.

Red picked her up and carried her to the living room. He was shocked at how light she felt in his arms. She had always been a petite woman but now it seemed even her bones were as fragile as a bird's wing. He settled himself in the big easy chair and held her on his lap, stroking her hair and massaging her shoulders. His mind went back to the many times he had held Penny in this very same way, soothing away real and imagined hurts or real and imagined slights.

Kathryn's body went limp against him and she broke into uncontrolled sobs. "I'm sorry, so sorry ... " she gulped between sobs. "You must think I'm a terrible person; I just need to feel warm again, to feel something, anything!"

Strickland felt his own body respond to hers and wrapped his arms around her more tightly. But even as he stood up and lifted her, still cradled in his arms, he knew that if he gave into this temptation at this time it would spoil forever whatever might happen between them in the future. He set her carefully on her feet and turned her to face him. "Now, Kathryn," he said, giving her shoulders a little shake. "I want you to go into the bathroom and wash your face and comb your hair. I'll be in the kitchen, heating you a bowl of that soup and making us both some coffee. After you have some of the soup, then we'll talk."

She took a long time before joining him in the kitchen. Her hair was pulled in an untidy knot at the back of her neck and her face was washed but still bore the evidence of her tears. "I'm so sorry, Red," she whispered, taking a seat at one end of the table. "I don't know what came over me. Before you rang the bell, I was sitting in the dark, seriously thinking of ending my life. Now I almost wish I'd done it before I made a total fool of myself with you."

Red set a bowl of soup and a cup of coffee in front of her. "You don't mean that, Kathryn," he gently chided, taking a seat across from her and sipping some of his own coffee. "What didn't happen between us now isn't because I don't want it. But I don't want it when you're only trying to prove something to yourself. When I take you to bed it's going to be because it's what both of us want and at a time when we are loving, not just proving something."

Kathryn dropped her gaze and took a tentative spoonful of the soup before answering. "I feel like such a fool," she said. "If I promise to behave, will you stay with me for awhile?"

Red laughed in spite of the seriousness of the moment. "Of course I will," he said, looking at her over the rim of his cup. "I think we've both learned something tonight," he went on. "I've spent way too much time being sheriff and father and not nearly enough time realizing just how short life can be. When all this is over, and it will be over some day, we'll have this little talk again."

After Kathryn had finished her soup, Red rinsed the bowl and their cups and put them in the dishwasher. "Now," he said, "let's go to the living room and talk." They sat on the loveseat and again he held her to him but more in the way he so often had held his daughter. The kisses they exchanged now were almost chaste but they both knew a line had been crossed, a barrier breeched and that one day they would be able to share a life together.

It was nearly 2:00 a.m. when he entered his own house. Even with all the horror of the past few days he felt that somewhere in the future things would be much brighter.

TUESDAY

On the day of the funeral, the sky was gray and threatening, like the moods of most of the town's inhabitants. Red awoke with the feeling that there was something obvious about the murder of the Bannah students that he was overlooking. He hoped the snow would hold off until after the funeral. There was no question of burying the children today. That would have to be put off until spring when the ground had thawed sufficiently. He knew the funeral would be an ordeal to get through, both for the children's families, as well as for their school mates and everyone else in this close-knit community. He wondered as he showered and shaved, if the idea of a mass funeral had been such a good one. So much grief all centered in this one location at this one time. Perhaps it would have been better for each of the children's funerals to have been held in their respective churches.

Penny's mind was also on the funeral as she sat across from her father at breakfast. Mrs. Cooley did not mention the up-coming event, but was also subdued. Even Boots refrained from his usual morning begging. Penny felt he was tuned into the mood of the house.

"Do you want to ride to the services with me?" Mrs. Cooley asked as she and Penny cleared away the breakfast dishes.

"No thanks," Penny said. "Paula and some of the other kids are coming by for me. I talked to Mrs. Wilkins on Sunday and she said she thought it would be nice if all the classmates sat together."

"I'll see you after the services, Kitten," Red said, as he left the house. He planned that he and Charles, as well as the two night shift deputies, who had volunteered to work overtime, would station themselves at various points in the high school auditorium and keep their eyes on everyone in attendance. Perhaps, just perhaps, there would be some sign, an expression, an act, something out of place. He doubted that his luck would be that good, but he had to try everything he could think of. He felt somehow the whole gruesome thing was not over yet and if he did not manage to find the killer … He suppressed that thought as unprofitable and started the car, backed out the driveway and went to the school.

The Bannah high school auditorium sat five hundred people. Today all the permanent seating was filled, and permission had been given by the fire chief to bring in extra chairs. Those were also filled and there were still clusters of people standing here and there. The six coffins stood at the right on stage, banked behind with sprays of flowers. To the left, behind a speakers stand, sat members of the school board, Principal Tuttle and members of Bannah's clergy. The family mourners were all seated in the front rows, with the senior class and remainder of the students and faculty in rows immediately behind them. The sheriff was gratified to see that some of the instructors who had left for the holiday after school the previous Friday evening had returned for the services. He wanted to be sure to speak to them before they left town again.

He walked to the front of the auditorium so he could speak to the Reed family. "I called on you Saturday, but you weren't home," he said, placing a hand on Raymond Reed's shoulder.

"We went to Bismarck, to leave Maggie with friends. I didn't think she needed to be here during all this," Ellen Reed murmured.

"Ellen, Ray, I'm so sorry," Red said, taking Ellen Reed's cold hands in his.

She raised red-rimmed eyes to him and just shook her head.

"I'll want to talk to the two of you sometime soon," Red said, releasing her hands. "I know it's going to be an intrusion and a terrible thing to ask but I think I'm going to need to look through the rooms and belongings of all the kids involved."

"What do you hope to find?" Raymond Reed asked, raising his voice and glaring at the sheriff. "Surely you don't think our kids did anything to cause this horror to happen?"

"Ray," the sheriff replied, placing his big hand on the other man's shoulder, "I don't know what to think . . . I don't know what I'm looking for . . . but I'm grasping at any straw I can find."

Ellen Reed put her hand on her husband's other arm and looked at Strickland with tear-filled eyes. "Of course, we'll do anything we can to find out who did this," she said softly. "I'll begin going through Sandy's things as soon as we get home. If there is any scrap of evidence that will help you, we'll want you to see it."

Her husband gulped audibly. "I know you're only trying to clear things up, Red," he said, huskily. "It's just so hard . . ." He broke off and buried his head in his hands.

Red left them then and walked a couple of paces, stopping beside James and Molly Easter. He was shocked at the shrunken, aged appearance of the couple. Their eyes were red and swollen and their faces had taken on such lines of sorrow. He sat down beside them and put an arm about Molly's shoulders. "I tried to stop by to see you Saturday," he began, "to ask a favor . . . but the snow hampered my trip."

"What is it you need?" James asked, clearing his throat. "We've done little else other than try to come up with anything that would account for our boy's death along with the deaths of all those other poor children."

"I don't know if you've had a chance to go through any of Jim's things," Strickland began. "But if there is anything, maybe notebooks that might contain mention of something unusual going on, anything he might have been reluctant to share with you because he didn't want you to worry."

Molly met his gaze with tear-filled eyes. "I've done that," she said. "You know boys, committing anything to paper would be the last thing they would do. If they thought there was a problem, they'd try to handle it themselves."

"And do you think there might have been such a problem?" Red asked, turning toward her, feeling hopeful.

Molly shook her head. "No," she said. "The children James was mostly involved with were those he had started school with. His main interest was basketball and the rest of the time he just wanted to help his father with the farm."

Strickland thanked them and after expressing his regrets yet again, walked across the aisle to where Ted Campbell's parents sat huddled in their seats. 'Huddled,' was the only word he could think of to describe the way they looked.

"Jack, Anne," he said, shaking hands with the two people. "Where are the girls?"

"We didn't think this was the proper place for them," Jack Campbell said. "Carrie Abbott is watching them until we are finished here."

Anne Campbell dabbed at her eyes with a small handkerchief and returned it to her lap. The handkerchief looked damp and well-used to Red. "The girls don't really understand about what happened to Ted," she said. "They still want Christmas and Santa Claus and it's difficult to explain to them that Ted is with God now." At that point she broke down completely and her husband took her into his arms, patting her shoulder and talking soothingly to her.

Strickland left the couple. There was nothing more he could say or do; and, nodding to the other families as he passed them, he returned to the back of the auditorium where he could keep an eye on as many people as possible. It was time for the service to start.

Betsy Klein pushed past Paula Whitedeer so she would be seated at the opposite end of the row which she had entered. She wanted to keep her eyes on certain people. She had written her stories and had gotten the advice she had asked for. However, she was not sure the advice was what she had wanted to hear. She still would have to make up her mind if she wanted to take any further chances. Maybe, just maybe, she should tell Penny's dad what she knew, suspected rather, than take a chance. Well, maybe after the funeral, maybe tomorrow. Maybe she should show him the movie rental cards. Now she wondered why she had gotten herself into this in the first place.

Deputy Whitedeer had taken a position at the side of the stage, where he could carefully observe the people in attendance. That was his task, watch the audience, not the service. He saw grief, but also anger on the faces of the usually placid townspeople. He would have to be careful, when the crime was solved, to remind Red that lynching in a situation like this could not be overlooked.

Sam Tuttle scanned the sorrowful faces of the students from his prominent seat on stage. The flash of Betsy Klein's glasses obscured her eyes from him, but as he glanced in her direction, inspiration struck. Of course, she worked for the movie rental people. Who else would have access to his file? But what he rented from the movie people was surely no worse than what dozens of other people rented. He saved his more specific appetites for those movies he could purchase in secret. But his caller had to be Betsy Klein!

Len Jacobs watched the mourners as they filed in and filled the seats. He had a good view from his back row seat. He could name almost every individual in the place who took tranquilizers and/or sleeping pills. Why half the people in Bannah, including himself, could be found in one or the other of those categories. He searched for the face of Sunday night's caller. Sure he and Bill watched some kinky movies. Didn't everyone? He wondered why someone would think movies were linked to the murders. He'd have to discuss it further with Bill after the funeral.

Lynn Christman watched both the students and the faculty. Her eyes moved about the auditorium restlessly. She sought a face and wondered if he, too, would be in the crowd.

II

When the funeral finally ended, some of the people stood around outside the auditorium, waiting to see more closely or give their sympathy to those families who would be leaving the scene last. Penny and Paula did not wait. Penny had gratefully accepted a ride home.

"I looked at everyone I could think of," Paula said, her foot resting on the brake as she carefully backed the car out of the school parking lot. "I still can't believe that the kids were killed by someone we know."

"I know." Penny stretched her leg out as best she could, trying to get into a comfortable position. "I don't feel safe answering the door when I'm home alone. I even caught myself wondering about Mrs. Cooley!"

Paula laughed. "That is taking it a bit far, I'd say."

"Oh, you know what I mean," Penny turned to face her friend. "These are people we have known all our lives. I know some of the kids in school are a little weird, but I can't believe one or more of them could have pulled off something like that. If you discount the kids, then it leaves the adults, our parents, our teachers, our neighbors!"

Paula pulled into the Strickland driveway, stopped the motor and leaned her chin on her hand, looking at Penny thoughtfully. "I guess I never quite thought of it like that. Back on the reservation and in the Indian school, you didn't feel like you really knew people. We Indian people don't show our emotions very readily. We hide ourselves behind masks, a habit we cultivated in a white world, I guess. I could wonder about someone on the reservation. But here even someone in your dad's department . . ."

Penny shivered. "I don't think I even want to think about that one," she said. "Come on in and have a cup of cocoa."

"Thanks, but I guess I better be getting back home. My brother will be coming in for lunch before too long and I like to have something hot for him on the table."

"Do you like what you're doing?" Penny turned and asked on impulse.

"Like what?"

"Oh, I don't know, going to school here, keeping house for your brother. You don't mix a lot with the kids for the most part. Aren't you lonely?"

Paula opened the car door and stepped out. "I think I'll have that chocolate after all," she said.

The two girls greeted Mrs. Cooley who was just taking a load of clothes from the dryer. "Didn't you go to the funeral?" Penny asked, surprised.

"No," Mrs. Cooley said, beginning to fold the clothes onto the work table in the utility room. "I'll see the families later, when all the hubbub dies down and they will need some company and someone to think about them. I'll leave the looking to the lookers."

"We came in for some cocoa," Penny said. "I'll fix it. Then we're going to my room, okay?"

"Of course, Dear." Sarah Cooley watched the two girls as they went to the kitchen. She felt a tightening around her heart. How she had wanted to plead Penny's case with Red last Friday. Thank God she hadn't!

When the two girls got to Penny's room with mugs of steaming cocoa and a heaping plate of brownies, Paula took up her conversation as though she had never stopped talking. "I'm not sure if I'm happy or not," she said, helping herself to one of the brownies. "I really don't know where I belong, on the reservation I felt out of place. Most people don't want to do anything there. The Indian school made me feel inferior, talked down to, I guess, and I didn't like that either. Then I came here for high school. I thought things would be different."

"How?" Penny mumbled around a mouthful of brownie.

"I don't want to sound conceited or anything. I think I'm pretty bright. I always feel like the teachers are surprised that I get the grades I do, like an Indian shouldn't."

"I don't feel like that," Penny said, sipping her cocoa and trying to keep Boots from helping himself to her brownie.

"You're not a teacher."

"Maybe . . ." Penny didn't know how to continue. "Maybe you expect them to expect less from you. Maybe it's more in your head than in theirs."

Paula smiled and offered a bite of brownie to the cat who had given up on his mistress's generosity. "I feel like I have to try harder."

"I thought it all came easy for you."

"Just ask my brother how many nights I stay up way past midnight, cramming for a test or studying some trig or poem in lit."

"You come across very confident . . . and . . . remote, like you really don't like us a lot and don't want to be friends."

Tears came into Paula's eyes so suddenly that it surprised her as much as it did Penny. "I don't feel like that," she said, digging into her sweater pocket for a handkerchief. "I'm sorry. I guess it's all we've seen today."

Penny stood and impulsively put her arms around the dark-haired girl. "I hope you'll always want to show your feelings around me!"

Paula smiled. "Maybe the rest of this term won't be so bad after all."

III

While the girls were getting to know one another better, Red and Charles were still keeping a wary eye out for anyone acting unusual in the crowd. Red smiled and waved as Lynn Christman got into her car, but she didn't appear to see him.

"Was that a snub?" Charles grinned.

"Just preoccupied, I guess," Red said.

"She doesn't mix much with the rest of the teachers."

"But, according to Penny, she's one of the best teachers they've got."

"I know, Paula thinks so too."

"Know much about her?"

"Not really, I think she came from St. Paul or somewhere like that. She must not go back on vacations or anything. She is here all summer."

"Any one back there for her?"

"You mean like brothers and sisters? Not that I ever heard her talk about. Maybe I'll ask some time."

The sun was bright but there was no warmth in it. The two men watched as the parking lot slowly cleared. "I should really go see the Campbells and Easters," Red said. "I need to get them to go through Ted's and Jim's things and I hate it that damned snowstorm kept me away from them on Saturday."

"Why don't you wait until tomorrow. They'll have scads of people around them now."

"You're probably right," Strickland said. "I talked to both families and they seem to have already thought of everything to look for." He beat his fist on the steering wheel. "I don't know much we can do on this today. I just feel so damned helpless!"

"You've had every deputy beating down nearly every door in town," Whitedeer observed. "Something's got to break soon. In the meantime, let's just take it easy the rest of the day and get ready for what comes."

IV

Betsy Klein hurried home from the funeral, changed clothes and grabbed a few bites of lunch. She could get lots more hours in at her movie rental job during her Christmas vacation, and she sure could use the money.

"What time will you be home?" Betsy's mother called to the slamming door.

"Probably around ten," Betsy called over her shoulder. She planned to offer to lock up the store so she could make another phone call. She had seen Mr. Tuttle looking at her during the funeral. She wondered if any of the other people she had called had made the connection to her. Now the only thing that really linked her to those calls was her stories.

V

The sheriff sat behind his desk and shuffled the papers concerning the case. Many tools—he hesitated to call them weapons—had been used to dismember the bodies, but nothing that didn't exist in every household. He almost wished the kids had been shot. At least there would be bullets to help them identify the murder gun, but an axe, a kitchen knife, and a meat cleaver? He couldn't very well go from house to house demanding to see all these items and then check them for possible blood stains. Or could he? It would certainly take more manpower than he had. He decided to go home and, clicking off the light, closed the office door. He didn't know that the search for tools that he contemplated would already be too late.

VI

By the time for Movieland to close, the sky was overcast once more. A brisk wind had begun to blow, and snow scratched at the windows, demanding to be let in. Betsy pulled on her coat, stepped into and fastened her snow boots, tucked her small notebook with names of movie renters and lists of their movies into her pocket, turned out the lights and stepped outside the store, locking the door behind her. When she had gotten fully outside the shelter of the doorway and felt the full force of the wind in her face, she wished that she had driven to work instead of walking. But she had read that walking was the best exercise in the world; and God only knew, she could use a little exercise. She crossed the street and turned toward her house, into the full force of the wind. As she trudged through the already deepening snow, a car drew up beside her.

"It's too cold to walk," the driver said, motioning to the passenger door. "Get in and I'll run you home."

Betsy paused at the curb. She didn't want to appear ungrateful but didn't know whether accepting this ride would be a good idea or not. As she stood and considered refusing, an exceptionally hard gust of wind blew swirling snow into her face and down her coat collar. That decided it!

"I guess it will be all right," Betsy said as she slid into the passenger seat. "Hasn't the weather turned awful?"

"Many things have turned awful, Betsy," the driver said as the car pulled smoothly away from the curb. In the glow from the dashboard,

Betsy looked at the driver who was wearing a heavy vinyl raincoat that covered everything from neck to ankle. Before she could say anything, the car turned the corner in the opposite direction to her home and sped up. She saw in the driver's eyes, illuminated by the eerie glow from the dashboard, that she had made a big mistake. In that sickening instance, Betsy knew she should have trusted her instincts and not accepted that ride.

WEDNESDAY

It was 12:30 a.m. Red turned off the reading light above his bed and soon fell into a fitful doze. The shattering ring of the telephone brought him to a sitting position before the ring had died away. "Yeah," he barked into the receiver.

"Chief, this is Bob Daniels at the office. Mr. Klein just called us. Seems Betsy didn't come home after leaving her job this evening."

"Maybe she went somewhere with friends."

"They already checked all the places she might be. Helen Sanders who owns the movie rental place said Betsy volunteered to lock up for her so she took the afternoon and evening off."

"I'll get dressed and be down there as quick as I can," Red said and hung up before his deputy could say anything else.

As Red started down the hall, the door to Penny's room opened and she stood there, looking more than ever like a little girl, in her bare feet and long, pink flannel granny night gown covered with frolicking little white lambs. "I heard the phone," she said.

"I've got to go down to the office for a bit," Red said, hurrying past her.

"Daddy, Is something else wrong?"

"I hope not. Go back to bed."

Red had already grabbed his gun belt from his own closet door and now hurriedly put on coat and boots, noting the whistle of the wind outside, and the way the snow flakes began to fall faster and thicker. *Why do these things have to happen in the winter,* he wondered, getting into the car and hoping it would start without problems.

Later Red and Deputy Daniels began their search for Betsy, driving slowly along the route from her house back to Movieland. When they reached the store, Red was surprised to see that there were still lights on.

"Maybe she went back for something," Daniels offered as the two men left the car and walked to the door.

"Let's hope so," Red said, rapping on the door's glass pane. There was no answer. Red turned the door handle and was surprised when it swung in quietly at his touch. "Betsy," he called, advancing into the room and looking about him. "Betsy, are you here?"

Only silence greeted his question. "Maybe she's in the john," Daniels offered, walking toward a door at the back of the room.

"Wait," Red said; he drew his gun, and after knocking and receiving no answer, cautiously opened the door which led into a small bathroom.

The room was dark. Red's nostrils caught the sharp, coppery odor of warm blood. He ran his hand along the wall opposite the door until he found and flipped the light switch. Betsy's body lay slumped in front of the toilet. The room was small and had only that fixture and a small sink in it.

Daniels pushed forward and looked around Red Strickland's arm. He quickly turned away and put his hand to his mouth. He had not seen the mutilated bodies at the first murder scene, so was not prepared for the brutality of this murder. Betsy lay on her back with her head lying on the commode's base. Her body was nude. Both hands had been severed at the wrists. Her tongue had been cut out and lay between her ample breasts which had been slashed terribly.

"Go get the fingerprint stuff and camera from the office," Red told the young deputy, more to give the man a chance to get out and collect himself than for any other reason. "While you're there, call Charley, tell him what has happened and that I want him here on the double. Tell the dispatcher to call in the day shift early, each man to report as soon as he can!"

After Daniels had left the building, Red began making a careful search of the store, looking but touching nothing. Betsy's coat was hung neatly on the coat rack. Her clothes were in a heap as had been the clothing of the six victims, and lay on the floor next to the coat rack. He returned to the main room. It didn't look as though anything had been disturbed, but he wanted to know that for certain. He went out to the car, called the dispatcher and had himself patched into a telephone call to the Sanders residence.

"Hello!" Helen Sanders answered on the first ring, and Red knew they had not gone to bed for worry over Betsy.

"Helen," Red said now. "We found Betsy."

"Where?"

"In your store. I'm afraid she's dead."

There was an audible gasp from the other end of the line. "How?"

"I can't tell you that right now," Red said. "I don't want you to come down here for awhile, not until we've checked for fingerprints, and had the body removed. Also if you and Jack would drop by my office in the morning, we need to take your fingerprints as well."

"I understand," Helen Sanders said. "If there's anything else you need..." Her voice trailed off and Red heard the gentle click as she hung up.

He waited long enough for the dispatcher to disconnect the call and then he had him patch another call to the doctor's house. "Hate to get you up at this time, Doc, but we've got another one."

"Oh my God! Who? Where?"

"Movieland, Betsy Klein."

"I'll be right there."

A patrol car squealed to a sliding stop outside the door. Bob Daniels and Charles Whitedeer entered the store. Bob began methodically taking pictures of the entire store. He hesitated at the door to the bathroom, but then entered and took pictures of the body from every angle. When he had finished, Red asked him to begin dusting for latent fingerprints. "There's probably not much point in printing this main room," he said, "but I want every inch of that bathroom printed. Just maybe we'll get lucky."

When the dusting of the surfaces had been accomplished, Red began examining Betsy's clothing. "I don't find a key to the door," he said to the two deputies who now stood observing him. "She said she'd lock up, and from all I know, Betsy was a responsible worker, so presumably she did lock the door, yet it was unlocked when we got here."

"What about her purse?" Charles asked. The leather-like shoulder bag hung on the hook next to where the coat was hanging.

"You through with this, Bob," Red asked, pointing to the purse. Receiving a nod from the deputy, Red took a pen from his own pocket and carefully lifted the bag off the hook by its strap. Then when he had set it on the desk before him, he used the point of the pen to insert into the zipper hole and unzip the bag. Finally, using the pen as a lever, he upended the purse and emptied its contents out onto the desk top. "No keys here either," he said. "She should have at least had a house key. More than likely she kept the work key and whatever other keys she had on one ring. I'll have to find out from her folks if she had anything special on that ring."

Charles walked back to the bathroom door and stared at the body. "Why do you suppose her tongue was cut out and where are her hands?" he wondered aloud.

"According to Penny," Red said, "she was probably the biggest gossip in town. I'm sure it was symbolic."

"Paula would agree. I don't think lots of kids liked her too well . . . but still . . . this? Her hands . . . symbolic too?"

Red rubbed at his chin. "She wrote and she talked. She must have known something about the killings." He went to stand by the door, looking out into the blustery night. "She shared that knowledge," he continued, still staring out the door, "and it got her this! Doc Hardin's on his way. Help him with whatever he needs. I guess I better go up to the Klein house before they get the idea to come down here to look for Betsy."

II

He smiled grimly to himself as he began cleaning up the mess in the basement. He was grateful for the drain in the middle of the floor. Betsy had had a lot of blood but at least by draining most of it, her body was lighter for her transport back to Movieland.

Now he set the nozzle on the hose to full force and flooded the basement's floor. The stupid little bitch thought she was so smart. He wondered though how she had learned his secret. Well, that was one secret that had cost her dearly. That wagging tongue and those fat hands would never cause anyone any trouble again, especially not him. Now he was safe.

After making certain most of the water and blood had been swept down the drain, he trudged up the stairs. It had been a long and exhausting night.

III

When Red pulled up before the Klein home, he noted that every light in the house was on. Before he could even climb out of the car, both Kleins were standing in the front doorway. Red waved them back inside. Mrs. Klein looked at Red's face and burst into hysterical sobbing. Joe Klein took his wife's arm and led her to the sofa. "Better tell us, Sheriff," he said, seating himself beside his wife and holding both her hands.

"I'm afraid your daughter's been killed," Red said, seating himself in one of the arm chairs, without waiting for invitation.

"Killed? How do you mean, accident?" the Kleins asked nearly in unison.

"I'm afraid not," Red said. "She was in the building where she works, in the bathroom."

Mrs. Klein jumped to her feet and started for the door.

"Nancy! Where are you going?" Her husband looked alarmed.

"To bring my daughter home," Nancy Klein shot back over her shoulder.

Red Strickland was older but faster than Joe Klein. He reached Nancy just as she opened the door to leave the house. "Not now, Mrs. Klein, I'm afraid. The doc needs to see her and we need to have the place as undisturbed as possible to see if there are any clues."

"But I want my little girl home!" Nancy screamed, struggling to get free of the sheriff's strong arms.

The two men finally got her seated back on the sofa and fairly subdued. Joe excused himself and went upstairs. In a few minutes he returned with a glass of water and two pills in his hand. "Take these, Dear," he said, "They will calm you."

"I don't want to be calm! I want my daughter!" The woman screamed and began struggling once more.

After once more being subdued, Nancy Klein finally agreed to accept the pills. In a few minutes she sat silent and glassy eyed, her hands lying limply in her lap. She leaned against the back of the sofa, giving the appearance of a limp rag doll.

"What were the pills?" Red asked.

"Valium, Doc prescribed them a year or so ago."

Well, another Valium user, Red thought. Perhaps Len Jacobs was right. Half the people in Bannah were on some kind of sleeping pills or tranquilizers.

When they were certain that Nancy was not going to cause any more problems, Joe, with the sheriff's help, carried her upstairs and put her to bed.

They returned to the living room where Strickland remained standing, looking around the well-furnished room. Again there was the ubiquitous Christmas tree, its lights reflecting off the many colored ornaments and lighting the artificial snow banked at its base, supporting a mound of gaily decorated gifts.

Klein sank into a chair. He knotted and unknotted his shaking hands and his jaw trembled as he tried vainly to fight back tears. "Tell me, Sheriff," he said. "What happened to my little girl?"

"It's not pretty, Joe," Red said softly. "She was badly mutilated."

"Like those other kids?"

Red nodded. "I hoped you would be able to tell me why. Do you mind if I have a look in her room?"

"Up the stairs, first door on the right. Want me to come too?"

"I don't think so. Nancy needs you more. I'll call you if I have questions."

Betsy's room was much like the room of any teenaged girl, Red thought. Pictures of rock stars and movie stars decorated the walls. There was a good stereo system and a small color television in the room. He had never indulged Penny to that extent. He believed some things, like television and good music, should be shared. Penny did have a small clock radio/tape deck in her room for the kind of music Red simply could not stand to listen to for very long but the good stereo and the only television were in the living room. Red believed that children who were allowed to hide themselves in their rooms and where little communication with other family members was required, were the kids who got into trouble.

Now he sat down at Betsy's desk and began looking through drawers. He noted the many notebooks filled with stories, either completed or in the process of being completed, that Betsy had been writing.

He shuffled through a stack of the notebooks. *THE PRINCIPAL DID IT* jumped out as a title on a notebook at the bottom of the stack. Red picked it up and quickly scanned the pages. He saw that Betsy had begun a story, using the events of the past weekend as her main theme. A slip of paper with several telephone numbers marked the place where the story had ended. Red held the paper in his hand, and continued to read. The high school principal in Betsy's tale had kinky movie ideas. Red wondered if Sam Tuttle also had kinky movie preferences.

He pocketed the list of phone numbers and then continued his search of the room. Looking through some of the other notebooks, however, he found that Betsy had also begun scenarios where the history teacher, the pharmacist, and even the sheriff's deputy had done the murders. Was she fishing or did she know something, he wondered.

Methodically he went through the drawers of her dresser, her chest of drawers and the night table beside her bed. When he opened the closet door and began looking at the contents of the shelves above the rows of jeans and sweaters, sweatshirts and dresses that crowded every space on the metal rods, he found still another notebook. This one bore no title. He stacked it with the others and secured the group with heavy rubber bands he found in the middle drawer of the desk.

A brief glance at the first few pages of the last notebook had sent a shiver down his spine. This story told of a girl who had inadvertently learned a terrible secret involving someone looked up to and trusted in the community. The girl wanted an unspecified something. So she was wondering about either blackmailing the person involved or taking her information to the sheriff. She felt sure the information would lead to the solution of a particularly brutal crime which had recently occurred. Red wondered if this had been the case. Had Betsy learned something through her job at the movie rental store? Had she then attempted blackmail? But then why the stories involving the principal, the pharmacist and various other people in town?

Red sighed and turned to leave the girl's room. He took the notebooks with him. He would have to see what reaction Betsy's stories would have on the persons about whom they had been written. He would begin with Sam Tuttle. The clock on Betsy's night stand said 2:25 a.m. It was going to be another long day. He turned off the light, closed the door and went back down to the living room.

"I wasn't able to find Betsy's keys at Movieland," he said as he accepted his coat and hat from Joe Klein and walked toward the door. "She did have her own house key, didn't she?"

"Yes," Joe said. "Let me think a minute . . . She had the house key, her school locker key and the Movieland key on one of those key chains that beeps at you when you clap your hands. I think it was a big lady bug or something like that . . . I remember there'd be a shot on the TV or a door would slam and that thing would start to beep in her purse."

"That's very helpful," Red said. "By the way, I found this bunch of Betsy's stories in her desk. I know you won't mind if I take them along. They just may be of help in this whole mess."

"Betsy's stories?" Joe was startled and grasped the sheriff's arm. "What have Betsy's stories got to do with any of this?"

"I'm not sure yet," Red admitted, "maybe nothing, but there is a possibility that Betsy may have known something, or at least suspected something."

"Oh God!" The tears he had held back to that point came at last. "My little girl . . . what are we going to do?" He beat his fists, one into the other, and finally broke down completely.

The sheriff put his arm around the shoulders of the grieving man and slowly guided him to the chair he himself had so recently occupied. "When Doc Hardin's done with . . . with taking care of Betsy . . . I'll send him up here," he said. "Joe, believe me, I'm so very sorry about all this , so very sorry." He left Joe Klein sitting in the now grief-shrouded house.

IV

When Red Strickland returned to the Movieland building, he found Ben Hardin and a deputy just loading Betsy's body into the ambulance. "What did you find, Doc?" he asked.

"She wasn't killed here."

"I kind of had that idea," Red said. "There wasn't enough blood for all this mutilation."

"She was probably killed outside and then brought here, maybe not long before you got here."

"Why," Red asked, leaning against the doorway. He wished he had become the town's garbage collector instead of sheriff. Then he smiled ironically. When he caught this pervert, he *would* be the town's garbage collector.

"Something amusing, Red?" The doctor asked, stepping back into the building.

"Not really," Red said. "Just a private little thought."

"Well, as I was saying," Ben continued, "There's a surprisingly little amount of blood here. I think she was killed where it was very cold. Then maybe stuffed into a car trunk or something and brought here."

"But there is no blood on her clothing. Surely the guy didn't undress her and do all this out in the snow."

"I think he took her somewhere he thought safe, then undressed her and did the rest."

"But you can't just transport a nude body from here to there without someone seeing something," Charles Whitedeer objected.

"I think when we examine the inside of her coat, we'll find there is plenty of blood there."

"Why bring her here?" Charles asked.

"She had the keys. The place was closed for the night. Where better?" Hardin challenged.

"I may have something," Red volunteered. "We'll check it out first thing in the morning. Now, Doc, if you don't mind, after you get Betsy to the morgue, go over to the Kleins. Mrs. Klein took some pills, but she and Joe are both in pretty bad shape. They will both need some attention before morning."

The doctor nodded curtly and left the building.

"What about fingerprints?" Red asked. "And where's Bob?"

"He went back to the office to check what we got."

"Anything promising?"

"There weren't too many prints in the bathroom, considering; but who knows."

"Well, tomorrow morning we're going to start printing everyone involved with this case."

Charles Whitedeer raised an inquiring eyebrow.

"I've got stories here that Betsy wrote, implicating Tuttle, Hein, Jacobs, and even you, along with God only knows who else as our murderer. Betsy could have confronted these people with something she knew or at least something she thought she knew."

"And one of them killed her?"

"It's possible. Helen Sanders is going to check in the morning to see if any files are missing," Red told Charles as they walked toward Red's car. "I assume you left your car at the office when you came into town."

Whitedeer stood with his hand on the passenger door to the sheriff's car. His face was grim as he said, "I want you to know I had nothing to do with any of this and Betsy didn't contact me about any of this, if blackmail was what she was angling for."

"Good Lord, Charles," Red said, laying his hand on the other man's shoulder, "you are one person I hardly consider a likely suspect."

"Thanks for that vote of confidence, Chief. Do you think movies have got something to do with all this?"

"Kinky movies maybe," Red said as the two men pulled into the parking lot of the town hall. "The way all these killings were done makes me think that maybe we've got someone in town who likes to watch slasher movies."

"They just did this to see what it was like, like I said about those two guys, Leopold and Loeb?"

Red shook his head. "I don't think so," he said. "I think the reason lies much deeper than that, but the movies may have inspired the means."

"Why deeper?"

"Too much rage," Red said. "Whoever is doing this has a hatred in them the likes of which we've never seen before."

Later, Red drove toward his own home, his thoughts drawn to Lynn Christman. He wondered what Lynn could possibly tell him about Betsy's stories. From what Penny had said, Betsy had always been sharing her writings with the English teacher. Perhaps Betsy had told her something of the secret she had uncovered. He would have to call on her tomorrow and see. He also remembered that he had not yet inquired into Lynn's background, another thing for the morning.

When Red looked at his bedside clock in the morning, he was surprised to see that it was already after 8:00. He had only intended to rest an hour or so before returning to the office. The wind howled around the eaves of the house, and driving snow made skittering noises as the wind whipped it against the outside wall. Mrs. Cooley and Penny were already in the kitchen by the time he had showered and dressed.

"What was the phone call, Daddy," Penny asked, setting the table and stopping to fill his mug with coffee.

"Betsy Klein was murdered," Red said, drawing up his chair and sliding into his place at the table.

The plate Mrs. Cooley had been filling for him shattered as it struck the floor. "My Lord!" she gasped, "another one like the other kids?"

"More than likely," Red said, getting up and retrieving the broom and dust pan for Mrs. Cooley.

"When and where did it happen, Daddy?"

"Sometime between the time Betsy left her job last night and about midnight," Red said, accepting the new plate of food Mrs. Cooley set before him. "I don't know where it happened, but it was made to look as though it happened in the movie rental place."

Mrs. Cooley poured herself a cup of coffee and sat down without taking any food. "You just spoiled my appetite for the day," she said. "When is this all going to end?"

"I wish I knew," Red said, absent mindedly tossing bacon to the begging cat. "I have a lead to follow up this morning. Penny, did Betsy give you any idea that she might suspect any certain person of the killings?"

"I never talked to Betsy that much," Penny said. "She was the one who called and told me about the other kids, but she didn't say she had any suspicions. Besides, I don't think I've talked to her since. She didn't even say anything to us when we were at the funeral. She just kind of sat there and stared at everyone."

"What do you mean?" Red asked, pushing his plate aside. "Did you get a sense she had something on her mind?"

Penny left the table and stood at the sink, looking out the window. Then, without warning, she bent her head over the sink and began throwing up.

"Oh, my poor lamb!" Mrs. Cooley exclaimed, putting her arms around the girl's shaking shoulders. She took a towel out of the drawer, ran cold water on it and began sponging Penny's face.

Her father helped his daughter back to her chair. "I'm sorry," he said, kissing her cheek. "Maybe I shouldn't have told you like this."

Sarah Cooley began clearing the table, leaving father and daughter in their silent embrace. When the dishes were stacked beside the sink, she turned back to them. "Why on earth would anyone want to kill that silly little girl," she wondered aloud. "Maybe it's not the thing to say but that girl's always been an attention seeker from way back before she even started school. Her folks spoiled her rotten and gave her anything she wanted … but I can't believe anyone would really want to hurt her."

Penny drew away from her father and raised haunted eyes to his. "Do you think…er…she knew who hurt…murdered the others?" she whispered hoarsely.

Mrs. Cooley reclaimed her cup from the drain board and refilled it. She sat down heavily at the table and picked the cat up onto her lap, stroking him absent mindedly. "Do you have any notion where she was killed?" she asked.

"Not much chance," Red admitted. "It seems every time this monster decides to strike he waits for the weather to help him. There were no tire tracks outside Movieland when we got there last night."

"I really didn't like Betsy, much," Penny gulped, pushing her chair away from the table. "But I sure didn't wish anything like this on her."

Mrs. Cooley put the cat down and began to scrape the breakfast scraps into his dish. "What you need is a big dog," she observed, trying to lighten their mood a bit. "There's always too much leavings for just that cat."

VI

Strickland was glad he hadn't removed the chains from his car after the last snow. He drove carefully to his office and was pleased to see that Charles Whitedeer's car was already there.

"Bitch of a morning, Chief," Charles said, as Red walked in and tossed his coat on the back of his chair.

"What a greeting!" Red said. "You don't usually swear."

"Between the killings and the weather, a wooden Indian would swear," Charles said. "What's on the agenda?"

"Little trip to Tuttle's house, and then we'll hit everyone else we've talked to about this case," Red said, seating himself and picking up the phone receiver. After dialing a number, he listened for a moment and then depressed the button and dialed again. He repeated this same procedure three times and then gently replaced the phone receiver on its cradle.

"No one home?"

Red handed over the piece of paper with the telephone numbers on it that he had taken from Betsy Klein's notebook earlier that morning. "There were people home at those numbers," he said.

"Sam Tuttle?"

"And Bill Hein and Len Jacobs and . . . Lynn Christman."

At that moment the door opened and Millie Scott entered the police station, bringing with her a blast of frigid air and a swirl of blowing snow. "Sorry I'm late, Red," she said, shaking the snow from her coat and stamping the snow from her boots. "The snow was hell to shovel away from the garage."

Red filled her in on what had happened the previous night. "I've got something for you to do while we're gone," he continued, getting back into his own coat and pulling the flaps of his fur-lined cap over his ears. "Call around and see what you can find out about Lynn Christman, Len Jacobs and Bill Hein. See if you can get Mrs. Banning, the school secretary, to get the files for you. Then follow it up from there. I know it's hell with school closed for the holidays, but just do the best you can."

"What about Jacobs?"

"See what you can do about the two teachers first," Red said. "We'll see if we can find out where Jacobs went to school and about his past when I get back."

Millie Scott was pulling the phone to her as the two men left the office.

VII

The tires of the car crunched their way up the long hill to Sam Tuttle's house. "I know it wouldn't pay for the plows to be working now," Red mused, gripping the steering wheel hard. "I almost can't tell what's road and what's ditch along here."

"You don't really think Tuttle killed those kids, do you?" Charles asked, squinting through the swirls of snow blowing across the road. "He's weird, but a killer?"

"We'll see what he's got to say about the little story Betsy was writing. His reaction should give us something."

When they finally reached the Tuttle home, Red pulled the car to the side of the road and parked. "I wouldn't attempt that driveway with a jeep," he said, getting out of the car and waiting for Charles Whitedeer to fight his way through the drift from the passenger side. "Why didn't you just slide over and get out my side?" he asked, as Charles tried to dig snow from the tops of his high boots.

"Beats me," Charles grinned. "Stupid, I guess."

Sam Tuttle showed the two men into his spacious kitchen and offered them coffee which they both gratefully accepted. "What can I do for you on a morning like this?" he asked, returning to the table with his own mug of coffee.

Red handed him the notebook with Betsy's story in it. "Read this and tell us," he said.

Both the sheriff and his deputy watched Tuttle's expression as he turned the pages and read. "My God!" Tuttle said, handing the book back to the sheriff. "Did she give you this drivel?"

"Indirectly," Red answered, noncommittally. "Where were you last night between 10 p.m. and say midnight?"

"Right here, why?"

"Can you prove it?"

Tuttle's normally red face paled. "Do I have to?" he demanded, getting to his feet and beginning to pace the kitchen.

"Maybe," Red said, still not giving anything away. "Was anyone here? Did you talk to anyone on the phone?"

The principal returned to his chair. "Well, I wasn't here all the time," he admitted. "I wanted to check some records over at the high school and I left there about 10:30."

"Same question," Red said, "can you prove it? And," he added, "while we're on the subject of proving things . . . I didn't ask you if you happen to have a brown corduroy coat or jacket the last time I was here. Do you?"

"I think you'd better tell me what this is all about before I answer any more questions," Tuttle said.

"If you don't have anything to hide, then you shouldn't object to our questions," Whitedeer interjected.

"I called a couple of the teachers while I was at the high school," Tuttle said. "Miss Christman and Mr. Hein, if you must know."

"Why?" the sheriff asked, riffling through the pages of the notebook which now lay before him on the table.

"I wanted to check some student information," Tuttle said. A fine sheen of sweat had broken out on his forehead and upper lip and he mopped at his brow with the napkin he had picked up from the table.

"What students required checking on at that time of night?" Charles put in.

"Betsy Klein if you must know."

Red reached into his shirt pocket and produced the slip of paper with the telephone numbers on it. He handed it to Tuttle. "Recognize this telephone number?" he demanded, pointing at the top number on the list.

"Yes," Tuttle said, "It's mine. So what?"

"That piece of paper was in the notebook with Betsy's story. Did Betsy call you last evening?"

"No," Tuttle said, getting back to his feet and pacing now even more agitatedly than before.

"Then why do you suppose it was in that notebook with her story?" Red demanded.

"I don't know," Tuttle shouted. "Why the hell don't you ask her?"

"Because she's dead!" Red Strickland roared, getting to his feet and facing Tuttle squarely. The two men stood not more than a foot apart, looking like boxers who were about to square off.

The bluster went out of Tuttle as though someone had stuck a balloon with a pin. He turned and sank slowly onto the chair he had vacated. "*Dead!*" he gasped. His face was now suffused with purple.

Whitedeer got to his feet and began rummaging in the cupboard. He produced a glass and a bottle of brandy. Filling the glass with a generous portion of the brandy he handed it to Sam Tuttle. "Drink this," he ordered. "Then tell us the truth."

Tuttle took the brandy in two big gulps, then nearly choked as the fiery liquid coursed down his throat. "She didn't call me last night," he said shakily. "She did call me Sunday evening and again on Monday. She tried to disguise her voice. Said she knew things about me . . . er . . . movies I rented. She said I would find out who she was when she was ready. She hinted that my movie preference had something to do with the deaths of the other students. She said if I didn't co-operate, she'd go to you."

"Co-operate how?" Red asked.

"She needed some grades changed. She wasn't going to graduate, you see."

"So you killed her to keep her quiet," Charles said, softly.

"No!" Tuttle gasped. "You've got to believe me. I went to see how bad her grades were--that's what I was doing at the school. I called the teachers I mentioned to see how she was doing on her daily work."

"Then you left the school, picked her up at the movie rental place and killed her." Charles made the statement even more softly.

"How did you know it was Betsy if she didn't tell you?" Red fired at the nearly prostrated principal.

"At the funeral, I looked at her, and she was staring at me, really staring. I had suspected it was probably her calling Sunday night, and then, the way she looked at me, brought it all together. She worked at the movie rental place, and . . ."

"What about the movies?" Red interrupted. "You might as well tell us, because Helen Sanders is, right this minute, going through her files, and she will tell us even if you don't."

Tuttle's face blanched and then turned a sickly gray. "Girl movies," he whispered. "Nothing lots of other people around here don't rent."

"Why don't we have a look at your private collection?" Red said, getting to his feet. "While we're at it, we'll see about that coat. Where's your VCR?"

"No! Please, no!" Tuttle moaned, burying his head in his hands. "I get things . . . things you can't get to rent . . . I buy things . . ."

"Where?" Red thundered, taking the shaking man by the shoulder. *"Where are they?"*

Tuttle got to his feet and led the way to the huge bedroom which took up almost half of the second story of the house. Both Red and Charles stopped in the doorway of the bedroom. The walls were covered with pictures of children with children, men with men, and women with women, the acts these pictures portrayed were things that Red had only read about, never even imagined he would see in Bannah. There were piles of magazines under the king-sized bed, on the night tables and stacked on the floor. A twenty-five inch color television sat on a tall chest of drawers, and a VCR sat on top of it. Beside the chest of drawers was a cabinet nearly as big as the other piece of furniture. A key protruded from the cabinet's lock. Red opened the cabinet and began reading titles and information on the video cassettes that filled its shelves.

"Pretty heavy reading over here," Charles observed. He had seated himself on the edge of the bed and had begun thumbing through the stacks of magazines on the night table. "S and M, kiddy porn, you name it, it's here."

Sam Tuttle leaned in the doorway and said nothing as the two men methodically went through his room and the large walk-in closet adjoining it.

"You still haven't told us if you ever had a brown corduroy coat," Red demanded, after a thorough search of the closet did not reveal one.

Tuttle shook his head.

"Take tranquilizers or sleeping pills?" The sheriff asked.

"No," Tuttle said.

Red walked over to the man still leaning against the door. "Sam," he said, softly and sadly. "This isn't any time to lie to me. If you want a lawyer, you'd better call one. We already have the pharmacy records."

The principal began shaking, and had to be led to a chair. "Okay," he said. "I take Trazodone and Valium, and Tranxene. But I didn't kill Betsy Klein and I didn't kill those poor kids Friday night."

"Let's go back downstairs and get your fingerprints," Red said, helping him back to his feet and guiding the man down the stairs.

After Charles had produced a card and ink pad and the printing was completed, the three men sat in the living room.

"I'm going to get a warrant and search this house from top to bottom," Red now said. "That is, unless you don't have anything more to hide, and give me permission to search it now."

Tuttle sat, glassy eyed and stunned. "You've already seen all there is to see in my life," he said. "Look where you will. I've got nothing else to hide."

Without a word, Charles Whitedeer left the room. Red knew he would make a thorough job of the search. He turned back to the man. "Tell me," he said softly, "what do you think the parents in this town are going to say when they find out your taste in literature and movies?"

The principal seemed to shrink into himself and into the chair in which he sat. "Do you have to tell?" he whispered.

"Depends," Red said.

"I've never done anything to anyone," Tuttle mumbled. "I just look at pictures and watch movies. I have never done anything to the kids in school. I . . . I . . ."

"Yes?"

Tuttle buried his face in his hands and this time he wept softly. Finally he looked up and met Red's eyes. "I'm impotent," he whispered. "I've never been able to do anything with anybody. I tried it all: whores in Bismarck, male and female. Nothing turns me on, nothing *real,* just pictures."

Red watched the man's eyes carefully. "What about killing? Would that turn you on?"

Tuttle shook his head. "My dad drowned a batch of puppies once," he said. "A stray bitch came to our house. I wanted to keep her. My parents said animals were dirty and carried germs. I smuggled her into the garage and fed and played with her. Then she had puppies and my father found out I had kept her against their will. He took the little puppies and drowned them one by one in the toilet. Then he took a club and smashed the bitch's head . . ." Tuttle's face was gray now. His eyes brimmed with tears. "I was sick for a week," he whispered. "I hated my father after that. I don't even set traps for mice. I could never kill anything."

The sheriff felt sorry for this poor wreck of a man. He sighed deeply. The trail was not at an end. This man was sick; just how sick was yet to be determined. If the story he had just told was true, then he probably had not committed the murders. Red wondered if he could trust anyone any more. *The things we keep hidden from the outside world,* he mused to himself, and wondered what other dirty little secrets lay behind the otherwise innocent-appearing closed doors of Bannah. "Did anyone know about Betsy's blackmail attempt?" he asked.

"Not unless she told them," Tuttle said. "I said nothing about it, you know why."

"What about the story she wrote. Do you think she might have shown it to someone?"

"How could I know?"

"I'll see what her parents say," Red said, "also I suppose you don't mind if I check with Miss Christman and Mr. Hein about your calls?"

"No, I don't mind," Tuttle said. "I don't mind anything you do. Just please, don't tell the parents what you found here today. I'd lose my job."

The sheriff got to his feet and towered menacingly over the little man. "I should run you in, you know, Sam," he observed. "I won't do it right now but there is a price you are going to have to pay for this."

Tuttle looked up at him, once again drawing his neck as far down into his collar as it could go. "What are you saying?" he asked.

"I'm saying that you are going to resign your position as school principal," Strickland said. "You can claim poor health, too much stress after the murders or whatever else you like."

"You can't do this to me!" Tuttle blustered, his face turning scarlet.

"I not only can but will," Red barked. "You have one of two choices, Sam. Either you resign or I expose your dirty little secret. I only have your word right now that you didn't kill those kids and I'm not through with you by any means. But for now, I'm not taking you in...so you decide!"

Charles came back into the room. "There's nothing here that looks like a murder weapon, Chief," he said.

Strickland felt sorry for Tuttle, but not sorry enough that he didn't want to see him squirm. "What you've got here is a crime," he said. "Kids look up to you, Sam. You're supposed to be an example of what kids should grow up to be like. God forbid if that's the case."

The two men left Sam Tuttle still sitting, shrunken in his chair.

"Well," Charles said, this time entering the driver's door and sliding across to the passenger side. "What do you think?"

"I wish we could say it was all over now and that we had our man," Red said, starting the car and rocking it gently back and forth out of the rut in which it had settled itself. "I'm going to do some further checking. I'd really hate for the rest of this to become common knowledge. The poor bastard's really got a problem."

"But?"

"If there's a trial, this is all going to come out. Betsy called him and tried blackmail; but not just on him, remember that. This does tie in though with the girl who knew a terrible secret, maybe not the killing but all that porn would wipe out Tuttle's career for sure."

"So was that why Betsy was killed?"

"I don't know," Red admitted, maneuvering the car through the increasing piles of snow. "Maybe Helen Sanders can tell us something."

VIII

Paula sat at the kitchen table watching the snow swirling across the yard. She had *To Kill a Mockingbird* lying open before her, but she had stared at the same page for the past ten minutes. She was thinking of what Penny had said to her on the previous day. Maybe she had been too hard on everyone in Bannah. Maybe she'd also been too hard on herself. Perhaps her teachers and even her classmates had not really expected as much of her as she had blamed them for. Perhaps she didn't fit in either the Indian or the white world simply because she did not know to which world she wanted to belong.

Charles had told her, as they sat over breakfast that morning, about Betsy Klein's brutal murder. Paula didn't like Betsy, but she hadn't deserved to have her life taken. She wondered what Penny Strickland was doing just then, what she thought about all this. She got up from the table and went to the wall phone and lifted the receiver. *No,* she thought, replacing it again. She didn't want to make a pest of herself. Just because Penny said she wanted to be friends, was no reason to spend all her time at the Stricklands. Then she shook her head at herself and picked up the receiver again. It was thoughts like those which had isolated her in the past.

Penny was glad to hear Paula's voice. "Come over if you can make it through the drifts," she said. "I really want someone to talk to. I guess you know about Betsy."

"Yes," Paula said from the other end of the line. "Your dad followed Chuck over here a while ago so he could leave the car for me. I thought that was nice."

"Hurry over," Penny said. "I told Mrs. Cooley she had better go home early because of this storm. Why don't you bring some things over and stay the night? I'll call the office and Chuck can have supper with us."

"I really couldn't," Paula protested.

"Yes you can and you should," Penny argued. "Just hurry. I want to show you what I got Dad for Christmas, and you can help me wrap it."

Paula smiled as she replaced the receiver. There was a warm glow on her cheeks and the howling wind sounded now more like singing. Maybe making the first move wasn't so bad after all. She ran to her room where she gathered some night things and a change of clothes. Then letting Prince, the Beagle, out for a run, she returned him to the house and put him in the basement with ample food and water. She would tell Charles to make a trip home that evening to allow him another run. It certainly was too cold to allow the poor little thing to remain outdoors.

IX

Helen Sanders was waiting for the sheriff when he reached Movieland. "This is strange," she said, motioning the two men to chairs beside her desk. "I've gone through the receipts like you asked me when you called this morning."

"What kind of receipts do you keep?" Red asked.

"We have an index file of all our subscribers," Helen said, motioning to the wooden file cabinets behind her desk. "We also have records of what our patrons like to borrow and have borrowed in the past."

"Why's that?" Charles asked, looking interested.

"For one thing, the IRS," Helen said. "It helps with our income tax records and all."

"How long do you keep the files open?" Strickland asked, absently rotating his hat in his hands.

"Practically forever," Helen admitted. "We keep active files on our renters and once they have stopped renting for at least a year or we know they've died or left town, they go into an inactive file."

"Why the lists of what they rent?" Charles asked.

"We know what kind of movies to stock regularly that way. People make specific requests and we need to see just how often a particular movie is rented."

"Am I going to need a warrant to look at your files?" Red asked. "I hope not…but…"

Helen shook her head. "Not under these circumstances, Red," she said. "If anything in these files can help you find who has murdered Betsy and all those other kids, I have no problem with you looking at whatever you need to see."

"Is anything missing to your knowledge?" Charles now asked.

Helen shook her head. "No," she admitted, "but it seems that Sam Tuttle and some of our other leading citizens have some really strange movie preferences."

Red exchanged a look with his deputy. He still did not want to believe that Sam Tuttle had killed anyone. "Who besides Sam liked strange movies?" he asked.

"Some of the other teachers," Helen said, leaning back in her chair and running a hand through her short, dark curls.

"Can you give names?"

"Well, there's that history teacher and druggist who live together. They go in for some of the 'adults only' kind of things they have out."

"Sam Tuttle?"

"Oh," Helen smiled and winked. "His tastes were a little kinky, but no more so than lots of my customers."

"X-rated kinky?"

Helen chuckled softly. "You know, Sheriff," she said, "You'd be surprised at the upstanding citizens of Bannah whose movie tastes run to the bare and sexy."

"Tell us about it."

"Well, there are those who park across the street or down the block when they come in for a movie. They look over their shoulders to make sure no one can hear them, and then they kind of suggest without really saying the kinds of movies they would really be interested in."

"How pornographic do your movies run?" Charles asked.

"No porn," Helen said. "Like I said, lots of bare skin, lots of panting and bed scenes, but nothing X-rated even."

"What about gore?" the sheriff asked. "Who likes slice-and-dice?"

"Now there's a different story," Helen said, turning to her file drawer. "Of course, we're even limited in that regard. We go to R-rating. We get some of the movies that have had scenes that have been edited out, even for cable television, but most of the gore you can see at your local theater or on your very own TV."

"So, who gets gore?" Charles wondered.

Helen began thumbing through the file. "You'd better get a note book and start writing," she laughed. "Half the people in this file drawer liked Halloween, Friday the Thirteenth, Freddy Kruger—'see-how-many-people-you-can-kill-for-no-reason' movies. Even Miss Christman gets . . . um . . . some of our gorier offerings."

"Gee, thanks," Red said. "I don't know if we can convict anyone for watching gore or not."

"Unless they stop watching and start doing," Whitedeer put in thoughtfully.

"Hey, Charles," Helen Sanders said suddenly. "Here's your file. Want Red to have a look?"

The deputy's face turned a shade darker than normal. "I don't think so," he said. "It's really Paula who enjoys those scary things."

"Better stop before you get to Penny's file," Red laughed. "Hers is probably the biggest stack. But then he turned serious. "This isn't finding our killer."

"Any leads at all?" Helen asked, closing the file drawer and turning back to face the men.

"Not really," Red admitted sadly.

The two men left the movie rental place and returned to the office. "Penny called," Millie greeted Red as the two men walked in.

"You probably should have stayed home in this storm," Red said. "But I'm glad you're here. Has the Doc called?"

"Yes, he says for you to come on over to the hospital when you get a chance."

"What did Penny want?"

"Paula's going to spend the night at your place and the two girls are cooking supper for the two of you. Also, Charles, your sister says go let your dog have a run before you come over."

Red looked at Charles who showed some surprise. "Glad the two girls get on so well," he said. "Penny needs a steadying friend like Paula."

"I'm glad to see Paula reaching out toward someone," Charles admitted. "I've had the feeling she isn't very happy here, but she won't open up to me."

"What did you find out about Lynn Christman?" Red asked, leaning on Millie's desk.

"Not a lot yet," she sighed. "She came here two years ago. Her family is dead except for a brother and his whereabouts was not listed. They were raised by an aunt and uncle in Minnesota after their parents were killed. I haven't been able to check on her previous jobs or schooling yet."

"Good start," Red said. "Sounds pretty routine, but keep trying anyway. Anything on Hein and that Jacobs?"

"Not much. Hein was born and raised in Bismarck. His parents and two sisters still live there. Both sisters are married. He seems to have led a pretty normal life. No police files on him, not even a traffic ticket. Nothing really on Jacobs either yet. He's from around Detroit or Chicago or somewhere. I called our old pharmacist; but he's out of town for the holidays, so I probably won't be able to find out much until later."

"He should have his license in the drug store," Charles put in. "that will give us an idea of where he graduated. Maybe we can go on from there."

"Do you think one of them did it?" Millie Scott asked.

"They are all new people in town who have had definite dealings with the kids involved," Red said. "I know we may be on a completely useless hunt, but I can't help feel it is someone who dealt with the kids on a daily basis."

Blowing crystals of ice bit into the faces of the two men as they retraced their steps to the car. "Remember the year it snowed so bad the trucks couldn't get in with fuel or groceries and the theater was showing *Snowbound?*" Red asked, starting the car and pulling out into the street.

"I wasn't living here then," Charles said, "But I remember reading about it."

"Well, let's hope this isn't going to be a repeat."

"At least if no one can get in, it will keep lots of the reporters from coming back when they hear we've got another homicide, and, for that matter," Whitedeer added, "our perp maybe can't get out of town either."

"That's the only ray of sunshine I've seen today," Red admitted grimly.

The two men sat in Dr. Hardin's office, happy to be in the warmth. Ben Hardin opened the bottom drawer of his desk, extracted three paper cups and a bottle of scotch. "We all need this to keep the chill away," he said, pouring generous shots into each cup.

"Find anything interesting about Betsy?" Red asked, accepting the paper cup gratefully.

Dr. Hardin looked at the two men grimly. "I can't swear it," he said, "But her tongue was cut out before she was killed."

Red passed the paper cup back to the doctor and motioned at the bottle. "That needs another one," he said.

"What I think happened," Dr. Hardin went on, passing the replenished cup back to the sheriff, "is she was knocked out and stuffed into the car. Then probably while she was still unconscious, or after she was knocked unconscious again, her tongue was removed. Then the killer went to work on the rest of her."

"Are you saying she was conscious for the rest?" Charles gasped. He looked as if he might lose the liquor he had just swallowed.

"I think," Hardin said slowly, "that is why her tongue was removed. So she couldn't scream for help while she was being murdered."

Red shook his head. "The others were drugged," he said. "It wasn't as much fun for the killer to hack and mutilate them. They didn't know what was happening. He did that and it wasn't enough. He had to inflict pain when the person could feel that pain."

"You're describing a fiend," the doctor said.

"No, Doc," Red said sadly. "*You* described the fiend. I'm just recapping."

"I thought her tongue had been cut out to symbolize the fact that she shot off her mouth too much about the wrong people," Charles interposed.

"That was a bonus for the killer," Hardin said. "If that's what it looked like, it would send you in another direction."

"What about her hands? Was she alive for that too?"

The little doctor shook his head. "No," he said. "There was very little bleeding evident from the wrist areas, indicating her heart had already stopped pumping before her hands were removed."

"And the tongue?" Strickland asked.

The doctor looked grimly at the two men. "There was a considerable amount of blood in her lungs," he said, "indicating that not only was she alive but she strangled on her own blood."

The sheriff and his deputy both looked at the doctor, open mouthed.

"In God's name!" the sheriff exclaimed, striking his knee with his fist. *"What in hell are we dealing with here?"* After his outburst, he leaned back in the chair and stretched his long legs in front of him. "Got awhile, Doc?" he asked. "I've got another bizarre story for you."

Over the next half hour Red and Charles told him about Betsy's stories and their visit to Sam Tuttle.

Ben refilled the paper cups once again. "I've known Sam all my life," he said. "Now it seems I didn't know him at all."

"What kind of a childhood did he have?" Red wondered out loud.

"We both grew up here in Bannah," Ben said. "My dad was the doctor here, you know, and when I got out of medical school, I just kind of fell into his practice. When Sam and I were going to school here in Bannah, he wasn't allowed to have any friends. His parents thought their son was a few cuts above the rest of us; even doctor's kids weren't good enough for their Sam.

"So he came to school, did his school work, and went home. He never participated in sports. His mother didn't want him to get dirty, or hurt. Sam's parents had come to this country, hearing that anyone could grow up to be the President of the United States. They were sure their Sam would fill that role."

"Then why did he come back here to teach?" Red wondered.

"Good question. I think when they sent their little boy off to college, he found he was ill-equipped to function in the real world. He took the path of least resistance, got his education degree and came back to Bannah, where Mom and Dad could take him back into the protective shelter in which he'd grown up."

"But I seem to remember hearing they hated the fact that he came back," Red said.

"Right," Hardin agreed. "They made his first years back in Bannah a nightmare. They threatened to disown him, to make him move out and live on his own."

"Then what happened?" Charles asked, sipping meditatively from his cup.

"They died."

"How?" Red and Charles both asked.

"I'm not sure," the doctor admitted, leaning back in his chair. "They were pretty well up in years when Sam came along. I believe Mrs. Tuttle died of a coronary, and for a while it looked like both Sam and his father would follow shortly. They hadn't had to function before without a woman in the house. Old Tuttle died three months after his wife."

"Any chance either death wasn't natural?" Red asked, crushing the paper cup and tossing it into the wastebasket.

"Who knows." Harden made a face. "Nobody was looking for anything out of the way. The old lady had been in bad health for a while. Everyone assumed old Tuttle just went because they had been together so long he couldn't function without his mate."

"So Sam could have . . ." Charles began.

Ben gazed thoughtfully at the two men. "After what's happened here in the last few days," he said, "I wouldn't rule anything out, past, present or future. Sam never could relate to people. I don't think he ever had a date; and, from what you just told me, sex in general wasn't going to work for him."

The deputy shook his head. "Sad, in a way," he said.

"Betsy had to have told someone else her theory. Unfortunately, that someone was the killer," Red said.

XI

The sheriff and his deputy left the hospital. The blizzard had become increasingly strong, with snow obscuring their vision. "It's a good thing the rest of the town seems to be quite law abiding," Charles remarked as they got into Strickland's car.

"Who'd be stupid enough to commit a crime in this weather?" Red said, starting the car and turning on the defroster. "I'd be in by the fire if I had a choice. Right now it looks like I'm going to have to scrape this damned windshield."

"Let me," Charles said, already opening the door on his side of the car and reaching for the ice scraper. When he had cleared a sufficient space, he got back into the car. "Wonder what the temperature is?" he said, slapping the snow from his gloves.

"Couldn't you have done that outside?" Red laughed. "Now, do you want to flip to see who's going to see Christman and who's going to see Hein?"

"I saw Hein's car at the pharmacy. Just drop me there and when I'm done I'll go back to the office."

"You'll freeze your brains in this storm."

Charles looked down at his gloved hands. "I've been thinking," he began softly, "'bout all those packages under all those Christmas trees. I want to find something special for Paula."

The sheriff didn't argue. He dropped Whitedeer in front of the pharmacy and made his way to Lynn Christman's house.

She invited him once again into her cozy living room. There was a fire crackling in the fire place. She was dressed in blue jeans and a plaid flannel shirt, brown loafers on her feet. Red found himself thinking again how non-gender this woman appeared. On looking at her closely, he decided she was probably older than he had first guessed, at least mid thirties, maybe even older.

"Want coffee?" she asked, seating herself in the recliner.

"By the time this case is over," Red grinned, "I may give up coffee and tea permanently."

"Want something stronger?"

"No thanks. I just have a couple of questions I need answered. Did anyone call you last evening regarding one of your students?"

She raised a questioning eyebrow. "No," she said. "I don't think the phone rang at all last evening."

"Then tell me about Betsy Klein. What kind of a student is she?"

Lynn waved her hand. "So-so," she said. "She's interested in literature and English, so she does fairly well in my class. She wants to be a writer and I, of course, encourage her. But I think she spends a lot more time on her writing than she does on her other school work. Why do you ask?"

"Was she going to graduate?"

"As far as my classes were concerned she was."

"What about the other classes?"

Lynn ran her fingers absently through her short hair. "Unless there's a real problem, we don't generally discuss our students in that way. Oh we talk about them sometimes, such as a discipline problem with a particular student, but I really have no recollection of anyone saying anything about Betsy's grades. Again, may I know why you are asking?"

"Betsy was murdered last night," Red said.

Lynn's jaw dropped open. "Why?" She gasped.

"I'm not sure," Red admitted. "She was trying a little blackmail to improve her grades. Maybe it caught up with her."

"Blackmail? Whom?"

"I'd rather not say right now. You are sure no one called you last evening about Betsy's grades?"

"Positive," Lynn said, picking at imaginary lint from her jeans. "I was home all evening, no calls."

"Are you going home for the holidays?" Red asked in an abrupt change of subject.

"I have no home to go to," Lynn replied. "My parents have been dead many years and I have no other living relatives."

Strickland raised an inquiring eyebrow. "I thought . . . um . . . that you had a brother."

The teacher shook her head sadly. "I once had a brother," she admitted, "but he was killed many years ago."

"Why don't you spend Christmas with us then?" Red asked impulsively. Immediately he regretted making such a hasty invitation. Perhaps the teacher and/or his daughter would be uncomfortable, spending time together on a personal level.

"Thank you," Lynn smiled at him. "The Reverend and Mrs. Benton have asked me to spend Christmas day with them. I appreciate the offer anyway."

"If you can think of anything about Betsy that might help, please call me," Red said, getting ready to take his leave. Then almost as an afterthought, he turned back to the woman. "I'm sorry to have to ask this of you," he said, "but I will need to take your fingerprints."

The teacher stared at the sheriff. "Whatever for?" she demanded, backing away from him.

"We're retracing our steps," Red explained. "At the time the other students were murdered, we really had no reason for fingerprinting anyone in town. But now, considering that Betsy was . . . well, let's say found in a place where fingerprints might provide some help, we are fingerprinting anyone and everyone who has had dealings with Betsy and the other students."

The teacher sank back into her chair. "I've never been fingerprinted," she said lamely. "What will you compare my prints to?"

"The prints found where we found Betsy's body," Red said. "Believe me, Miss Christman, it's purely routine."

Reluctantly the teacher submitted to the taking of her fingerprints. The sheriff thought she showed relief when he again began to take his leave.

Lynn stood at the window watching the sheriff get into his car. She hugged herself and shivered despite the warmth of the fireplace. It was all too bizarre. He couldn't have, wouldn't have done these terrible things. She had been so careful to protect him, to keep him safe with her. He was no killer . . . not really…He would have no reason to…She would as soon believe herself capable of murder as to believe that he could have killed those children.

Red drove away thoughtfully from the Christman home. She said she had no relatives but Millie Scott had learned she had a brother. He wondered why she had denied that piece of information. Perhaps he really was dead and Millie simply hadn't unearthed that piece of information yet. Perhaps she felt it was none of his business.

XII

When Red got back to the office, he found Charles waiting for him. "Well?" he asked.

"Hein says Tuttle called him about a quarter to eleven last evening. Jacobs confirms it. He was the one who answered the phone."

"What about Betsy's grades?"

"She was failing most subjects. Hein says her head was always in the clouds. I called some of the other teachers, the math teacher, and the business classes teacher. They all confirmed what Mr. Tuttle said."

"I wonder why her parents didn't know this," Red wondered out loud, seating himself at his desk.

"Maybe they did."

"We'll have to find out," Red said. "Somehow though, I don't think so. Did either Hein or Jacobs object to the fingerprinting?"

"No, not at all," Charles said. "And I saw that Jacobs got his pharmaceutical training in Michigan. I've got a call into the police department there to see if there's anything they can tell us about him. By the way, I sent Millie home. There wasn't that much doing around here and the weather isn't getting any better."

"Want to hear something strange? Christman says Tuttle didn't call her last night. Why would he lie about that?"

"Gilding the lily, maybe," Charles said, tapping a pencil on his desk.

"What's that mean?"

"He wanted us to think he was really digging into things. So he called William Hein, got the answer he was looking for, so told us he had called Miss Christman too."

"It's possible, I guess," Red said. "He didn't say that Miss Christman told him Betsy was or was not failing. That could be an indication that you're right. But," Red challenged, "answer this one. She also said she had no relatives, specifically no brothers or sisters."

Charles looked at the Sheriff sharply. "If she lied about that . . ." he began.

"There might be a lot of reasons," Red found himself suddenly defending her. "She did say her brother died years ago so perhaps Millie just hasn't dug far enough to get us that piece of information. We'll have to find out though."

XIII

Paula sat at the Strickland kitchen table, frosting the two-layer chocolate cake the girls had baked earlier in the afternoon.

Penny stood at the stove, stirring a large pot of spaghetti sauce. "Would you believe," she said over her shoulder, "this recipe was my mom's?"

"Do you remember her?" Paula asked.

"Not really. Sometimes I think I dream about her and about things that we did when I was little. But then I wake up and everything is kind of right at the corner of my mind. In a few minutes I forget even that much."

"She's been dead a long time, hasn't she?"

"I was five, I think."

"My mom died when I was born. She was an alcoholic, I guess," Paula said, taking the knife and frosting bowl to the sink.

"What did you do then?"

"Well, Charles was ten when I was born. He was already living with a foster family here in Bannah and going to school. I stayed with my grandmother. Charles came back to the reservation from time to time. When I was ten, he was already twenty, and more like a dad to me than a big brother. I thought he was already really old."

Penny laughed. "Where was your dad?" she asked.

Paula sat back down at the table and looked at her feet. "I never knew," she admitted.

Penny felt a hot flush rise to her cheeks. "Get down from the top of the refrigerator, Boots," she said, to break the awkward silence. "If Mrs. Cooley catches you up there or catches me leaving you up there, she'll have both our hides." Penny picked the cat up and sat at the opposite end of the table.

"You talk to that cat just like he understands what you say," Paula said.

Penny rubbed her chin on the top of the purring cat's head. "He does," she laughed. "He's the only cat I know who loves pizza, spaghetti, green onions and tomatoes. I'm sure he was sitting on the fridge just so he could look into the pot to make sure I had made enough sauce."

"You've made enough sauce to feed Bannah," Paula said.

"You haven't seen Daddy eat spaghetti yet," Penny said, setting the cat on the floor. "For that matter, I don't do too badly at it myself."

Paula regarded Penny with a steady, penetrating gaze. "Do you think of them much?" she asked.

"Them?"

"The kids ... er ... our friends ... you know, from the hay ride. I can barely sleep for thinking about--wondering about--who could have done such a terrible thing."

Penny tented her fingers in front of her and regarded her friend. "I try not to, but... it's impossible not to. I dream about them...things we did through the years, then wake up and finally remember." Tears filled her eyes. She set the cat on the floor and walked to the window and gazed out at the ever-increasing storm. "I think it's going to be terrible when we go back to school and they just won't be there!" She brushed at the tears that threatened to spill onto her cheeks. "I'll even miss stupid Betsy Klein prancing up to Miss Christman's desk with another one of those awful stories."

Paula shivered. "I keep thinking about their murder. Do you suppose any of them knew what was happening?"

Penny resumed her seat and shook her head. "Maybe not with all the drugs they got. At least I hope not."

"Do you think Betsy was drugged?"

Penny rolled her eyes. "Daddy hasn't said anything," she finally admitted. "I sure hope so."

"Charles didn't tell me anything either, but I could tell he was pretty sick at what he had seen."

"There were lots of times I wished Betsy would drop dead, but you know we never really mean that when we think it. It's just something to say. I don't think I'll ever say it again!" Penny looked up at the kitchen clock and jumped to her feet. "I better put the spaghetti water on," she said, "a couple of hungry people will be here before we know it."

XIV

Before going to the Strickland home, Red and Charles paid another visit to the Kleins. They declined offers of coffee and seated themselves in the living room. "I've got some tough questions I need to ask," Red began after an awkward silence.

"I have one for you too," Mrs. Klein said. "Why haven't you caught this maniac whose killing our children? What are you and your men doing all day?"

"Nancy," Red said, "I know you're upset. Believe me, we are doing everything we can to find out who killed those kids. Now tell me something, how was Betsy doing in school?"

"Fine," Mrs. Klein said immediately. "Oh, she wasn't an 'A' student like . . . like some . . . but she got by. She was doing all right."

"Do you have her report cards handy? I'd just like to take a look at them if you don't mind."

It was Mr. Klein who went to the desk and extracted a packet of cards which he placed in the sheriff's outstretched hands. Red looked carefully at the cards. He couldn't be absolutely certain without closer inspection, but he was fairly sure some of the grades had been doctored, "F's" changed to "B's." But what did it matter anyway? Betsy wouldn't graduate, no matter what her grades had been. "Thank you," he said, returning the cards to Mr. Klein. "Now I'd like to go back up to Betsy's room. I would like to take some more of the stories that she wrote back to the office with me."

"No!" Mrs. Klein shouted. *"They are all we have left of our child. You can't have them!"*

"I'm not going to keep them," Red assured her. "You may have all of them back as soon as I've finished reading them."

"As I asked you before," Joe Klein said, "what do my daughter's stories have to do with these killings?"

"Perhaps nothing . . . perhaps they will tell us who killed her."

THURSDAY

It was nearly 1:00 a.m. After the sheriff and deputy dropped the story notebooks by the office for safekeeping, they had gone to the Whitedeer home where they took care of the Beagle's needs and then on to the Strickland house and enjoyed the meal of hot spaghetti and sauce the girls had prepared, then they washed the dishes for them. Now the four of them sat at the kitchen table playing Monopoly. "I better go home and see if the water pipes have frozen," Charles said.

"You just want to go because you're getting beat," Paula accused.

"I didn't say you had to come with me," Charles laughed.

Paula pushed her chair back from the table, but her brother laid a restraining hand on her shoulder. "Stay here, Sis," he said.

"Please stay," Penny added. "Charles can come for an early breakfast and then he and Daddy can do whatever it is they do."

"Thanks, kid," Red said. "I do what puts shoes on your feet and clothes on your back."

"Casts on my legs you mean," Penny laughed.

"No," Paula said. "You did that one yourself, besides it's a foot now, not a leg." Both girls, giggling, rose and began to clear the game pieces and coffee cups from the table. Charles was about to go out the door when the telephone rang. At almost the same instant the fire siren began to wail.

"Strickland," Red answered, after he had snatched up the receiver. He listened for a few minutes and then hung up. "Fire at the Tuttle place," he said, getting his coat and boots, and buckling on his gun belt. "I don't know how long we'll be," he said over his shoulder as the two men went out the door. "You don't have to wait up."

Penny and Paula went to the back of the house from where they had a good view of the hill on which Sam Tuttle's house rested. Red-orange flames shot several feet into the air. The top of the hill was as bright as day. "I can't believe all this is happening," Penny said as she and Paula stood with their faces pressed to the window from which they had cleared the frost.

"Do you think it's got anything to do with the killings?" Paula asked, agitatedly twisting a lock of her hair around her finger.

"I just keep thinking we'll wake up and none of this will be real," Penny sighed. "Let's finish clearing away the stuff in the kitchen. I sure am glad you're here."

II

Buzz Fox, the fire chief, met Red and Charles at the bottom of the hill. "Can't save it," he said. "The flames are so hot, and the house already had such a good start by the time we got here, there was really nothing to do. All we can do is watch that sparks don't set off anything down the hill."

"Got any idea about what started the fire?" Red asked.

Fox shook his head. "Something could have overheated," he said. "What with as cold as it's been, lots of people have their furnaces and fires going full blast. But right now, the fire's too hot to tell for sure. We'll just have to wait for it to cool down some before we know."

"Anyone seen Sam?" Red asked.

A quick canvass of the people who stood around watching the fire revealed that Sam Tuttle had not been seen.

There was really nothing more they could do. The on-duty deputies had the gathering crowd under control and the Fire Chief said that the fire was under control as well. So the two officers went to the deputy's house, where Charles opened various faucets, let the puppy out for another run and then returned him to the basement.

"What do you think," Red said as the two men sat at the kitchen table, both reluctant to leave the warmth of the house.

"Maybe Sam started the fire himself," Charles suggested. "Maybe ... maybe he's still there."

"I thought of that too," Red admitted. "Maybe I've been wrong. Perhaps Sam was our killer after all and this was his way of dealing with the whole thing."

"The poor bastard," Charles said. "If we do find him in the house, that's what the townspeople are going to think."

"Not necessarily." Red got to his feet and walked to the window where he looked out. "None of the townspeople know what we found this afternoon and now everything we found is nothing more than a pile of melted tapes and ashes. Also people do burn to death, especially in the winter like Buzz said; people may not think anything. Let's go back to the office and wait. He will report what he found and the night dispatcher maybe can use help with the questions. I doubt we will get any sleep now."

III

It was early morning, and the fire chief, still wearing his helmet and turnout coat, sat across from Red at the sheriff's desk. The blizzard had stopped but the sky was leaden and snow flurries hung in the air like fog. Plows flung huge piles of snow to either side of the streets as they labored through the drifts. Storekeepers added to those snow piles as they cleared paths in front of their respective places of business.

"The boys and I nosed around the fire again this morning when it had finally cooled down enough." Buzz said, accepting a cup of coffee from the sheriff and nodding his thanks. "We found a body and what may be evidence that the fire was no accident. Doc Hardin's got the body and a couple of my guys are looking after the other stuff."

"Suicide?" Red asked, moving some of the papers on his desk onto the large pile that was growing on the right side. He wondered if he would ever get the time to work on it. Then he settled himself with a note pad to hear Buzz's answer.

"We'll have to leave that up to Doc." Buzz took another sip from the cup in his hand. "He could have doused the place with kerosene all right. We did a pretty thorough sifting of the stuff," he said, lacing and unlacing his fingers as he spoke. "There was one kind of interesting thing."

The sheriff rested his chin in his hands and stared at the fire chief. "What was that?"

Fox reached into his pocket and extracted a plastic evidence bag which he dropped onto Red's desk. "Keys," he said.

The sheriff stared at a large key ring which consisted of a black and red lady bug and several keys of various sizes. He clapped his hands sharply and the lady bug emitted a weak chirp.

At that moment the door opened and Charles came in brushing snow from his shoulders. He then took off his hat, and shook the snow from it as well, before he hung it up.

"Come see what Buzz found. Uh, Buzz, you didn't say where you found this."

"In Sam's pants pocket," the fire chief said. "What's so important?"

Charles stared at the ring of keys still lying on the desk. "Betsy?" he asked.

Strickland gingerly passed the bag containing the ring over to his deputy. "Dust the keys for prints and then take it up and have the Kleins identify it," he ordered. "But I'm ninety-nine per cent sure it is hers and those keys will fit their house, Movieland, her school locker and whatever else she had keys for."

Charles took the keys and left the room.

Fox stared at the departing deputy, and then turned back to Red after Charles left. "We got all the hot spots cooled down," he said, "but I think you really need to get the state guys back. We need whatever expertise they can give us in determining just how that fire started. I'd also appreciate it if you'd send a couple of deputies up to relieve my guys, they worked the fire and are probably pretty tired. Anyway I got to get back."

"Before you leave, where'd you find Sam's body?" Red asked the departing Chief. "From the way that fire looked, I can't believe you found him in any shape to have pockets even, much less keys in them."

"That's funny," the fire chief admitted, turning back to face Red. "Somehow Tuttle's body wound up in the basement under a pile of debris. It's quite possible the fire got ahead of him and the kitchen floor collapsed, dropping him down into the basement and offering a fair amount of protection."

"Kind of freaky, isn't it?"

Fox shook his head. "The house was old and well built but the floor joists were old too," he said. "Until we know just where the fire started we can't say for sure but that's the most likely theory I can give you right now." With that comment, he left the office.

When the fire chief had left, Red sent some men to relieve the firemen and then pulled the telephone over and put in a call to Bismarck.

"You want us to come to Bannah today?" the Captain at the State Police office laughed. "It will take a dog sled and then some to get out of here even, let alone tackle a county road."

"What about a helicopter?" Strickland asked. "We really need someone here. We've had a suspicious fire and the school principal was killed in that fire, and," he added reluctantly, "we have a murder of another school kid as well. We were trying to keep it a little quiet to avoid the media circus we had last week . . . but. . . ."

"Say no more," the Captain said. "We'll get someone there if it does take that dog sled!"

"Might as well take off your coat," Red said as Charles returned to the office half an hour later, stamping snow from his boots. "What did the Kleins say about the keys?"

Whitedeer sat down and nodded solemnly. "They're Betsy's all right," he affirmed. "Her initials were scratched on the bottom of that lady bug. But, unfortunately, as far as fingerprints are concerned, it was wiped clean."

"I was afraid of that," Red admitted. "I made a call and the guys from Bismarck are on their way."

"You got them to agree to come with all this snow?" Charles queried, leaning against the sheriff's desk.

"With two more bodies and a questionable fire, they're hitching up the dog sleds," Red grinned.

"So," Charles asked, reluctant to leave. "Is it all over? Do you think Tuttle killed the kids after all?"

Strickland drummed his fingers on his desk. "Before this morning I would have said no," he admitted. "Now, with Betsy's keys in his possession and all..." He struck the desk with his fist. *"I wish I'd have arrested the bastard yesterday!"*

"Except yesterday wasn't soon enough," Charles said. He snapped his fingers as though a thought had just occurred to him. "Red," he began, "I went through that house yesterday. I looked in the basement and everywhere else. There was no sign of blood anywhere."

"So?"

"If Tuttle was really as squeamish as he led us to believe, where did he kill Betsy and what happened to all the blood?"

Strickland's shoulders sagged. His deputy was not sure whether it was with relief or fatigue. "I'll worry about the blood later," the sheriff said. "Right now more than anything I want to believe that Tuttle is our perp. We only have his word that he was squeamish. I'm betting all that child porn and S and M finally got to him and maybe he did make an advance on one of the kids."

The deputy nodded. "It all fits when you look at it that way," he admitted. "Then when Betsy came up with that little blackmail scheme of hers, he wasn't sure what one of the kids might have told her before he had a chance to shut them up."

Strickland stood to his feet and stretched his arms high above his head. "If we'd only searched Sam's house the first time we went to see him," he lamented. "At least one life might have been saved."

"It'll all have to come out, won't it?" Charles said. "The town's going to want answers."

Before Red answered him, the phone on his desk jangled shrilly.

"Strickland here." He listened in silence for a few minutes and then hung up, shaking his head. "Here we go again!"

IV

Charles waited patiently as Red put on his hat, coat and boots again and then followed him silently until they got to the car. "So what was the call?" he asked as they each opened a door and got in.

"I couldn't recognize the voice," Red said, putting the key in the ignition and pulling away from the parking lot, wheels spinning and snow flying. "Whoever the person was, said they had seen Donald Bennett at Tuttle's place about the time of the fire."

"Wonder how anyone saw anything in that near blizzard and what idiot would be wandering around at that time of night in the freezing cold?"

"Guess we'll find out." Red drove the car to the end of Main Street and then turned toward the Bennett house.

"Think Donald started the fire?" Charles asked, gazing out the window as they passed a yard full of children erecting a giant snowman.

"I don't know that Tuttle would have let him in," Red said, "but maybe Donald told him he wanted to talk about coming back to school."

As the car pulled up in front of the Bennett house and they got out, Charles looked around. "No one has shoveled anything," he observed. "But, of course, everything could have drifted back before the wind stopped."

The two men made their way carefully around the house to the back door. Repeated knocks on the door got no response. Strickland, trying the knob, was surprised to find the door unlocked. "Donald, Mrs. Bennett!" He called out. He entered, Whitedeer close behind, and was met with a blast of hot air that made the room stifling.

"God! How can anyone live in this kind of heat?" Charles looked around the spotlessly clean kitchen.

"There's a note," Red walked over to the kitchen table and looked down to read it, careful not to touch it.

I CAN'T TAKE NO MORE, the note read in capital letters, carefully hand printed. ALL THEM KILLINGS AND THE CALLS AND THE WHISPERS TELLING ME I DID THEM. I JUST DON'T REMEMBER DOIN' ALL THEM TERRIBLE THINGS. AND I KNOW NO ONE WILL BELIEVE IT AIN'T ME. SO I'M MAKIN' SURE MY MA AND ME DON'T GET NO BLAME.

The two men hurried toward the stairs that led to the bedrooms. Mrs. Bennett lay in her bed, neatly covered, as though peacefully sleeping. Red picked up her hand and it fell limply to the quilt. "It's so damned hot in here it's going to be hard to tell when she died," he said turning away from the body and hurrying to the next room.

Donald also lay on his back but he had no peaceful appearance. A .38 caliber pistol lay under his chin with his thumb still stuck in the trigger guard. He had placed the pistol in his mouth and death had obviously been instantaneous.

The two men looked at one another and Whitedeer shook his head. "No one is going to lie there while someone shoves a gun into his mouth," he said. "This one's really got to be as it appears, a murder and a suicide."

"I hope to God you're right," Red said. "Go out to the car and radio the office and tell whoever answers to get Harden over here."

In less than twenty minutes, the little doctor had arrived in the ambulance and two deputies followed him. "Where the hell is this going to end?" Harden thundered as he surveyed the carnage that once had been Donald Bennett. He opened his bag, put on some gloves and bent to examine the body more closely.

"I want every inch of this place searched," Red instructed the deputies.

"Do you think someone really saw Donald by Tuttle's house?" Bob asked, as he took pictures of the body from every angle.

"From what his note said, he had something going on, even if it was all in his head. Finish these pictures here and then get some in the old lady's room after Doc finishes in there. You come with me." Red motioned to Charles and walked out of the room, returning to the kitchen. Another deputy followed closely, carrying a Polaroid camera.

"I want this piece of paper fingerprinted," Red instructed, pointing to the sheet of lined paper that still lay on the kitchen table. "In fact, print the whole damned kitchen! Maybe someone else came here and found them and decided to use Bennett as the perfect scapegoat."

"But I thought we figured this was all Tuttle," Charles observed as he left the kitchen, heading for the sheriff's car and their fingerprint equipment.

The sheriff ignored that comment and instead asked the doctor a question as he followed them into the kitchen. "You done with Tuttle's autopsy yet, Doc?"

Harden shook his head angrily. "In case no one remembers, I'm also a medical doctor with a degree and all that and I've got live patients that need tending, too. What brought you out here in the first place?"

Strickland explained about the phone call stating that someone said they had seen Donald Bennett lurking around the Tuttle house at the time of the fire.

"The Tuttle house was clear across town," Harden observed. "How in hell did he get up there and back in near blizzard conditions and why?"

"I guess that's something we'll never know now," Strickland admitted.

"If he was up there and had called you, would you have believed him?" Bob Daniels asked, returning to the kitchen.

Strickland flung up his hands in surrender. "At this point I'd probably have believed him if he'd said he saw a coven of witches performing some kind of fire dance in front of Sam's house. This whole case just can't get any more screwed up or crazier than it already is."

"But there were no footprints," Charles objected, returning to the kitchen and beginning to dust for fingerprints. *"And can someone turn down this damned heat before the house burns down!"* He demanded.

"Maybe that's what someone was angling for," Red observed as he headed for the basement. "A nice little fire they couldn't set this time . . . but . . . if it started on its own . . . Daniels!" he bellowed up the stairs. "As soon as you can, get down to the basement and dust the furnace for prints." He went on down the steps and after taking a careful look about, went over and carefully turned off the old oil furnace that took up a good part of the Bennett basement.

Charles joined him. "Just look at this accumulation of *junk!*" he exclaimed. "There are enough old magazines and newspapers down here to set this place up like a roman candle!"

The two men left Harden and his attendant to figure out how to load two bodies in one ambulance and get them to the hospital morgue. The two deputies continued to search the Bennett house and outbuildings.

"I still don't understand why if it's a setup someone called us before the house had a chance to burn down," Charles observed as the two men returned to the office.

"Maybe we were just lucky," Red said. "If someone did see Bennett up there and tipped us off, at least we didn't have another fire to contend with. And if Sam was our killer then why the hell all this?"

"Bennett wouldn't have tried to set the fire," Charles observed. "If that would have been the case, then why leave a note?"

"I think it was simply so damned cold last night Mrs. Bennett probably raised the heat so the whole house would get warm. Then when Donald got home from his late-night rambles if, indeed, he was out rambling at all, and decided to do what he did, he wasn't worried about the heat."

"So you really think he killed his mom and himself?" Charles asked slumping into his chair.

"Like I said," Red admitted, "I almost hope that's the case. I feel like this town is ready to explode and two more murders might just make that happen."

He smiled to himself as he replaced the telephone receiver. Maybe he should have waited a little longer and maybe his week of late-night telephone calls to the Bennett house hadn't even produced the results he'd hoped for, but either way, Donald Bennett was screwed up enough now he might confess to just about anything and maybe, just maybe, he had taken the caller's final suggestion of ending it all before he ended up back in a padded cell or worse. He'd simply have to sit back and watch to see. He hadn't realized what pleasure setting this horrible little town into chaos would give him.

VI

Once again the Bannah senior class was assembled at a funeral. True, this was really more of a memorial service, but the Kleins had wanted the service to be held as soon as possible. Neither had any close relatives, and as Betsy's remains could not be buried until the spring thaw anyway, it was decided to hold her service on this cold, Thursday afternoon. The mournful bells of the Methodist church tolled seventeen times, Betsy's age at her death. Teachers sat on the side aisle of the church, the center being reserved for the family and students. The church was filled to overflowing, with many of the curious lining the sidewalk outside, hoping to get a glimpse of the bereaved family as they entered.

Penny found a seat next to Paula and squeezed the girl's cold hand in greeting. "Did you hear about Mr. Tuttle and the Bennetts?" she whispered.

Paula nodded. "I still can't believe it's possible that Mr. Tuttle killed Betsy and the others," she said softly.

Penny sighed and leaned closer to her friend. "And I really don't understand about Donald Bennett and his mom. Do you think maybe we've got it all wrong and maybe he killed Mr. Tuttle and set fire to the house?"

Before she could answer there was a rustling and she glanced back to see the Kleins entering the sanctuary. Everyone stood as the sad couple, clinging to one another, walked down the center aisle and took their places in the front pew.

As the people once again seated themselves, Penny whispered, "Please, Paula, will you and Charles join us for Christmas day?"

Paula looked into her new friend's eyes steadily. "I think we'd like that very much," she whispered, back.

Len Jacobs and William Hein sat with Lynn Christman between them. Len knew his presence at the funeral had not really been necessary. But then the Kleins had always been good customers, and he felt they needed the moral support. It was funny. All the insinuations about William and himself in the town, but no one ever had quite had nerve enough to make it a formal accusation. He wondered how long William could expect to keep his teaching job in this little town if anyone actually had the nerve to accuse him of being gay. It was true, gays all over were coming out of the closet, so to speak, and some of them were accepted. But Len doubted that the good people of Bannah were ready for a gay history teacher or a gay pharmacist and especially not living together. He wondered just how long he himself would be able to stay in business were they to go public with their relationship. He also wondered why Betsy Klein had been murdered. She must have known something, something perhaps having to do with her job at the movie rental place. He guessed she certainly could have told a lot about the kinky movies he and Bill rented. But then Mrs. Sanders could still blow the whistle on that. He wondered if their taste in movies would again make them suspect for the killings. He was sure it wouldn't be long before they found out. Why had that Indian deputy found it necessary to take their fingerprints? Nobody said much about how and where Betsy had been killed. Now there were rumors about the fire at Tuttle's home and the sudden deaths of Donald Bennett and his mother. *Where,* he wondered, *would this all end?* He straightened himself up in the pew and turned his attention to the pulpit at the front of the little church.

Lynn Christman looked at the faces of her students and shivered. She wondered, not for the first time, if she was not somehow responsible for what had happened to the children. He had protected her in the past, it was true. But then she had always protected him too, hadn't she? Hadn't she literally devoted her entire life to doing and being what he had wanted? Now it was obvious he was out of control and things were escalating. Oh God, she didn't know what to do about it. What about Sam Tuttle? Her head began to ache and pound. She didn't want to think about Sam, Betsy, or any of them . . . but the thoughts spun around and around and she could do nothing!

Red sat down beside Kathryn Nye and took her cold hand in his. "Will you spend Christmas day with us, Kathy?" he whispered.

The corners of her mouth turned up in a tiny smile. "Yes," she whispered. "I . . . I think that would be lovely."

VII

After the service, a little group consisting of Red, together with Charles Whitedeer, and Buzz Fox met the State Crime Lab men at what remained of Sam Tuttle's house. "Surprised you could get here after all that snow," the sheriff said to Jerry Singer, the tall, blond man who had also been at the Easter farm investigation.

"We came in on the tail of the snow plows," Singer answered. "If that snow had kept up much longer, you people could have kept all your killings 'til spring."

The state crew followed the fire chief as he pointed out to them what he and his own men had found that morning. Samples were collected from various parts of what remained of the burned-out structure. "There's no doubt this fire was set," Singer said, coming back to where Red and his deputy stood. "If it was supposed to look accidental, the person sure didn't know what they were doing. There appears to be nothing subtle about your perp. My guys will get what they can to support that when we go to court. Let's head for the morgue and see what your pathologist's come up with."

The hospital corridors were quiet and nearly empty as the procession of men entered the morgue. "I'm almost afraid to ask," Strickland addressed the doctor, "but have you had time to do the autopsies now?"

"Oh yes indeed," Harden said, "and you aren't going to be happy with what I found." He went to a refrigerated locker and drew out a drawer. Red noted that despite the intense fire which had all but leveled Sam's house, the body of the man himself showed little damage.

"Mistakes were made this time," Harden explained as the men gathered around the corpse. "Remember, the house was old and the floor joists maybe weren't as strong as they should be."

"Meaning?" Singer asked.

"Too much of the accelerant was used in the kitchen area," Harden went on as though he hadn't been interrupted, "before the fire had a chance to do real damage to Tuttle's body, the floor apparently collapsed and sent him down into the basement. Then, and again here we were lucky, part of the floor collapsed on him and, as you can see, the body is not in bad shape."

"You were right, then, Buzz." Strickland said, and filled everyone in on what the fire chief had speculated.

"Couldn't he have started the fire himself and had this happen?" Charles asked.

The little doctor smiled grimly and like a magician about to pull a rabbit out of the hat, he turned Sam Tuttle's body over and pointed to the back of his head. "He was shot before the house was set on fire," he announced triumphantly.

"Then not suicide," Red declared.

"Not unless he was a contortionist," Harden agreed. "As you can see, he was shot at the base of the brain, a feat a little hard to pull off yourself."

"So any ideas about what happened?" The sheriff walked around the table so that he could see the body from all angles. He turned to face the others in the room with a fierce scowl. "So there goes the idea that Sam was our killer!" he spat angrily.

"Sam had a visitor I presume," Hardin said. "Sam probably offered his visitor coffee or something, and, as they sat talking, the person got up, walked around behind him and shot him."

"Well, at least you've got a fairly normal murder pattern for a change," one of the crime lab men observed. "From what we've seen around here and heard you folks don't do things by halves."

"Did you find the bullet?" Charles asked.

Harden nodded and went to a file drawer and extracted a small bag. ".22 from what I can gather," he said, handing the bag to Strickland. "As you know, a .22 isn't very accurate except at close range and this little bullet stayed right in the middle of Sam's brain."

"Now if we can just find the gun," Red said.

"We'll sift those damned ashes if we have to," Buzz Fox observed; "but I'll swear right now there was no sign of a gun anywhere in that house."

"What about the Bennett autopsies?" Red asked.

"Pretty straight forward," Harden said, sliding the drawer back into the cooler and leading the men from the room. "As far as I can tell what we saw is what we got. Donald smothered his mom and then killed himself." He shook his head as he stood with the men at the hospital entrance. *Maybe Donald's demons have finally been laid to rest,* he said to himself as he watched the others walk away.

Later, helped by the deputies and some of the firemen, the crime lab people began a methodical raking and sifting through the remains of the burned-out house. "We'll probably be able to tell you both the type of accelerant and just how it was distributed when we get this stuff back to Bismarck," Singer said as the Bismarck officers got into their four-wheel drive vehicle. " Give us a day or so and if I haven't called, you call me. Sorry to hear it looks like you're right back where you started as far as finding your killer though," he added. He shook hands with the sheriff and climbed in the vehicle which slowly pulled away from the curb. The drive back would probably be as slow as the drive to Bannah.

FRIDAY

Christmas Eve dawned bright and cold, the snow having stopped again, sometime during the night. Red swung his feet out of the warm bed and then sniffed the air. The entire house was redolent with the smell of baking. He stumbled to his bathroom where he showered and shaved.

Reaching the kitchen, he found Sarah and Penny already hard at work baking Christmas cookies and putting the final touches on the fruit cakes that had been ready since last fall.

"It's not even light out yet," Red said, pulling up a chair at the table and sipping the coffee Mrs. Cooley had thoughtfully pored.

"May I have the car today, Daddy?" Penny asked, reaching for a mug from the kitchen cabinet and filling it with steaming coffee.

"I really don't think you're ready to drive yet," Red said. "The streets are still slippery and you don't want a repeat of that cast, do you?"

"But I've got to deliver these fruit cakes and cookies to the shut-ins, Dad."

"I'll drive her," Mrs. Cooley volunteered, retrieving a pan of cookies from the oven and placing them on the rack to cool.

"Why not see if Paula can help with driving and delivery," Red suggested. "I like that girl. I think the two of you are good for each other."

"What about Charles?"

"I'll call him and tell him I'll pick him up this morning. Then Paula can have their car and come over when she gets ready.

Penny smiled at him. She had busied herself now cracking eggs into a bowl and adding milk and seasonings. "I guess you want scrambled eggs, don't you?" she asked.

"From the amount you're scrambling, I guess I'd better," Red laughed. "But how about a taste of one of those cookies first?"

"From the list Penny has for deliveries, you'd better see if there are any left," Sarah laughed, handing him an undecorated cookie from a mound on the counter.

"Looks like there's enough cookies and fruit cakes to feed all of Murray County," Red said. "But you aren't going to deliver *plain* cookies, are you?"

"Oh, Daddy," Penny said, pouring the eggs into the pan which had been heating on the stove. "When we get done with these cookies, they'll be the prettiest things you've ever seen. Why don't you tell Charles to send Paula over as soon as she's up. She can help decorate cookies too."

"Charles says you invited the two of them over for Christmas," Red said. "Will you have anything under the tree for them?"

"I took care of that yesterday afternoon, after the funeral," Penny said, the animation leaving her beautiful face.

Red was instantly sorry that he had made her remember the horrors of this past week. "I'm glad," he smiled now, accepting a plate full of eggs. I might have known you would handle things."

"That's sad about poor Sam Tuttle," Sarah said from the sink where she was wiping off the rolling pin. Was it an accident?"

"I'm afraid not," Red said. "I didn't want to bring this up at home, but you both may as well know. Sam was shot and his house torched."

"Oh, Daddy!" Penny gasped, *"who would want to kill Mr. Tuttle? I thought…uh…"*

Red nodded. "Yes, that he was the murderer. I think we all hoped that was the case because then this nightmare would have come to an end." He helped himself to another cookie and then took a sip of his coffee. "We had a long talk with Sam on Wednesday," he began. "Maybe Sam got to thinking about something we said after we left. Maybe he tried to check something and didn't realize what he was dealing with."

Sarah busily rolled out another mound of cookie dough, which Penny then expertly cut with various holiday-shaped cookie cutters. "Sam and I grew up together, you know," Sarah said over her shoulder.

"No, I guess I didn't know you had lived here that long," Red said.

Mrs. Cooley shot him a look. "Meaning I'm so old?" she laughed.

Red winked at his daughter who had seated herself across from him. "No," he said, "meaning I thought you were considerably younger."

"Go on with you now," she laughed. "But seriously, Red, I was first surprised that Sam went into teaching science. He was so squeamish when he was a boy. Experiments made him physically sick when we were in school."

Red raised an eyebrow. Then Sam had not lied when he told the story about the puppies. "He obviously got over it," was all he said.

"Maybe not," Penny objected. "He never really helped when we dissected frogs and things. Generally he stayed out of the lab on those days and would assign one of the kids to monitor the progress."

"But he had to do all those things in college before he would be a qualified teacher," Red objected.

"Well, I don't know about that," Penny admitted. "Maybe once you've done one frog, you don't have to do any more."

Red motioned Sarah to sit in a chair at the table. "Thought you two might as well also know that Donald Bennett really did kill his mother and himself. He left a strange note implying that some voices were telling him he had killed your friends and I think he felt we would lock him up."

"What made you go out there in the first place, Daddy?" Penny asked.

"That's another strange thing," Strickland admitted. "Someone called and said they had seen Donald up by Tuttle's house at the time of the fire so we went out to ask him some questions."

"So maybe he did do the murders?" Sarah wondered out loud.

"It would have been a great set up," Red admitted, helping himself to yet another cookie. "The problem is he killed himself with a .38

and Sam was shot with a .22. I've got Buddy Schmidt out there going through the Bennett house with a fine toothed comb seeing if there's another gun around."

"I've known the Bennetts for a long time," Sarah said. "Donald was a strange boy, full of anger and suspicion and his ma coped as best she could. I remember when they took him off to Jamestown. He'd been hearing voices and threatening to kill his ma and himself. I thought he'd settled down with the medication and all when they finally let him come home."

"Maybe all this just got to be too much for him," Red observed. "Maybe he stopped taking the medicine. He left a note and Ben Hardin says it's pretty straight forward."

"I can't take much more of this, Daddy," Penny sobbed. "I thought this was the safest place in the world. Nothing ever happened here. I wanted to get through school and go to the big city. *I wanted action! Now I just want my nice, quiet Bannah back!"*

Red left the table and put his arms around his daughter's shaking shoulders. "I know, Kitten," he said. "I always thought this was a pretty safe little town myself."

"Oh, I almost forgot," he said, leaving the kitchen to get his coat and boots. "I've asked Kathryn Nye to join us for Christmas Day too. Will that be a problem?"

"Oh no, Daddy," Penny smiled through her tears. "I'm glad . . . I miss Marcia . . . and . . . well . . . I like Mrs. Nye . . . Oh, Daddy, I'm going to take some of the cookies and fruit cake to Miss Christman," Penny added, retrieving toast from the toaster and buttering it. "You don't think she'll think I'm trying for any favors, do you?"

Red shook his head. "She knows you're a good student. She told me you and Paula are the brightest kids in her senior class."

Penny's face blushed with pleasure. "What are you going to do today, Daddy?"

"I should be in the office for the most part. Why?"

"Well, we probably won't have time to fix lunch," Penny said.

Red smiled. "I can see already I'd just be in the way around here. I'll grab something at the café. I'd hate to slow production for a mere thing like satisfying my stomach."

Mrs. Cooley looked and listened with pleasure to the father and daughter conversation. She knew Penny was trying to be extra bright and cheerful, despite the sadness the past few days had brought. At the same time, she knew that Red was doing everything he could to keep that brightness alive. "You come on home if you like," she said to Red. "I'll have something hot for you. The two young ladies can handle all this cookie nonsense."

"I'll appreciate your cooking all the more after a meal at the café," Red said at the door.

"Actually," Penny said putting on her most winning smile for Mrs. Cooley. "I think you should go home for the rest of the day. I'll have Paula here for company and I'm sure there are still lots of things you'd like to do at home."

Sarah Cooley smiled at her young charge. *But not so young any more,* she mused. Soon Penny would be graduated and gone. She hoped that there was some future for Red and Kathryn Nye. After all the lonely years of caring for their children, they deserved some happiness.

"Okay then," she smiled at Penny. "I'll help clear up these dishes and leave the rest to you and Paula. There are things I can do at home." Impulsively she gave the girl a hug and kissed her on the cheek. "If I'd had a daughter instead of all my big, rough boys," she said, looking deep into the girl's beautiful blue eyes, "I'd have wanted her to be just like you."

II

She had had a terrible night. The nightmare had left her shivering and sweating at the same time. She was back in her home, a child, maybe thirteen or fourteen years old. She had come home from school, breathless and excited. She was one of the finalists for the cheer leading tryouts. Her mother was not home and her father was at work. But her brother sat in the living room and smiled as she came in. Excitedly she told him her news. He looked at her, with a strange furtive look. "What's wrong, Larry," she asked.

He got to his feet and took her none too gently by the wrist. "Come with me," he whispered hoarsely. "I want to show you something."

"But you're hurting me," she protested.

He let up a little on the grip on her wrist and she followed him into his bedroom. "Now what is it?" she asked.

For answer he put his arms around her and kissed her full on the mouth. She drew back, startled, frightened; but also feeling a strange warmth and tenderness in her body. They were both mature for their age. Her breasts had required the wearing of a bra for the past two years; and she had already experienced what her mother called *the Curse* since she was ten years old. She looked at her brother who had grown to be several inches taller than she was over the past few months. He bent his head and kissed her again. This time he allowed his hands to roam over her body, touching her breasts whose nipples began to harden in response to the caress. He pulled her against him and she could feel his hardness against her.

That had been the beginning. At first he had been content to kiss and caress her. She found herself waking at night and remembering those kisses and his touch. As days and weeks had passed she found that she was no longer able to think of anything else. He had fanned a passion in her she had not known existed. Every day after school when they were alone, she had accompanied him into his room and they had satisfied their mutual hunger.

Time passed, they had become more and more reckless, and had crept into one another's rooms after their parents were asleep.

By the night of the fire, their illicit affair had been in progress for more than a year. She had just left his room and tiptoed to the kitchen for a glass of water when the fire had broken out. Their parents had died in the fire but she and her brother had been rescued. He had been badly burned. So badly burned, it was true, that for awhile doctors despaired of his recovery. But he had to recover. Her love for him . . . her need for him . . . was so strong, so all consuming, she would make him be well.

They had been taken in by her uncle, James Christman, and his wife, Peggy. She had stopped calling herself Donna Owens, and had taken her middle name, Lynn, and even though not legally adopted, had used the name Christman since that time. Donald Lawrence Owens had always preferred being called Larry to Donny. So all record of that previous life and the inferno that had almost destroyed their love had been erased.

But then Aunt Peggy had died and Lynn's uncle began taking special notice of her. She hated his looks, his touches. But when he came into her room one night and sat on the edge of the bed, she made no protest to the hand that ran exploring over her body. "It's not right," she whispered as he raised the sheet and slid his nude body in beside hers.

"I need someone," he whispered. "I need you . . ."

She felt miserable. There was no place to turn, no one to tell. She was still in high school with no place to go. But she could tell Larry, and she did and he said he would take care of her.

When it was all over, she called the police. She told them that her uncle had startled an intruder and the intruder had bludgeoned him to death.

"Where were you?" one of the policemen had asked, looking at her skeptically.

"He told me to hide in the closet when he heard the noise in the living room" she said. "No one knew I was home."

There had been an inquest, and the verdict had been death by person or persons unknown. Even the skeptical policeman had put a fatherly arm around her and offered comfort at the graveside service.

She had been placed in a couple of foster homes after that. Then came college, and she was once again able to erase the horrors of the past from her mind. Sometimes she wished she had not taken the Christman name, but then she thought perhaps one day she and Larry might return to North Dakota. She didn't want anyone there to remember the past. There were things . . . dark things that Donald Lawrence Owens whispered to her. Things that he wanted to do. She didn't think she really wanted her brother to accompany her if she went back to the Dakotas. Her past was too painful.

It was in her senior year of college that Frank Bates had come into her life. She really thought that she loved him. He seemed to be a gentle person who could make her forget her past. But then came the night of their graduation. They had been to dinner, dancing, and she had perhaps a few too many drinks. In the car Frank had become more insistent in his love making than he had in the past. "Why wait?" he demanded, fumbling with the buttons of her blouse. "As soon as I get a job, we're going to be married anyway. Honestly, don't be such a prude."

She told the police that a stranger had come upon them, there in "Lovers' Lane." Frank Bates was dead, horribly dead and she, herself, had barely escaped with her life, running through the woods where she had fallen and broken her ankle. The police believed her. Only she knew that her brother had found her once again. Even though their love was wrong, it was still the fire that ignited both their lives. She knew then that he would never let her take a lover, never let her marry and have a family. It would always be him for her or no one.

She had taught school first in St. Paul, then in Indianola, Iowa, then in Sioux Falls, South Dakota. All the time she was careful not to let herself become involved with anyone. She kept to herself, was a good teacher, and loved and protected her twin.

When she learned of the job opening at Bannah, she had been reluctant to take it. But Larry had urged her to try. He had wanted . . . had somehow needed . . . to be back where everything had begun. It was painful to see the lot, now with a grand brick house standing on it, where her childhood home had been. But twenty long years had passed since her home had been burned. The boys and girls she had attended school with were married, had children of their own, some of whom were in her classes.

She felt she loved these children, but she knew her brother did not. He had blamed the high school age and older boys, the sons of striking miners, for the fire and the loss of their parents. He felt the Sheriff had done little to see that justice was served. The arsonists had gone unpunished, had been allowed to live, to thrive and lead happy, normal lives. She shivered. Had he finally avenged their own ruined lives?

Lynn got out of bed shakily and took a shower as hot as she could stand it. She dressed in jeans and shirt and soft soled, brown moccasins and decided that today would be a good day for some general cleaning of closets, something she hated to do, and put off for as long as possible. After a couple of hours, she had only to clean the closet in the spare bedroom, his room. This one, she realized, would be the one to take the longest; therefore, she had put it off until last. This was the place where everything that had no place had been stored.

Twenty minutes later she sat on the bed staring at the contents of two large garbage bags. One contained a stack of video tapes, probably to be played on the VCR that sat on the closet shelf. The other bag contained clothes . . . bloody clothes . . . and in the top of the bag was a brown, corduroy jacket with one button missing.

Lynn Christman looked up, there stood her brother! "You did this," she whispered. "Why?"

"Because I love you," he answered. "There's only you and me. No one else matters." Then he took her in his arms and she felt herself melting into him and he was right ...

III

Red and Charles walked into the Station and hung up their coats. Red found himself wondering why they had bothered to come in on Christmas Eve, but here they were. After Red had picked up Charles and delivered Penny's message to Paula, the two men had driven to the burned-out ruins of the Tuttle house. After checking to make certain that nothing had been disturbed, they had decided, at last, to make their visit to the Campbell and Easter farms.

"I know we probably won't find out anything we don't already know," Strickland said, guiding the car along the rutted tracks in the country road, "but it is something that I feel needs to be done."

"Maybe they can shed more light on Sam Tuttle, if nothing else," his deputy agreed.

It was a long drive out to the Campbell farm, and the two men were surprised to see that there was little activity on the premises. The house looked shut up and still.

Red sighed heavily as he slid back in behind the wheel. "Looks like they decided to get away from here for awhile," he said. "Their car's not in the shed and it looks like everything's been shut up and turned off."

"I wish we could all get away too," Charles lamented, as the car began its way to the Easter farm.

Again Red was not totally surprised to find the house shut and everything quiet. But as they were about to leave, Will Lester came out of his apartment and down the stairs to greet the two men. "Mr. Easter decided he was going to take his wife to Florida," he informed them. "There's not much doing around here now and they said I could look after things until they got back. I'm also checking Mr. and Mrs. Campbell's place."

"And where did they go?" Charles asked.

"They've got relatives in Arizona," Will said. "Guess they couldn't stand having Christmas here, not even for those little girls, so they shipped some of the Christmas stuff yesterday and the girls will think for some reason Santa had to come to Arizona this year."

"When are they coming back?"

Lester shook his head. "I think if Mr. Easter had his way the answer would be never," he said. "I know there's no way they will be back until the holidays are over. Mrs. Easter is pretty close to having a nervous breakdown. And as for the Campbells, well, I guess we'll see them when we see them." With that he turned abruptly and began mounting the stairs to his apartment. Then he turned back suddenly and smiled at the two men looking up at him. "Oh yes," he said, "I got my nerve up and told Mavis about my jail time and all. She says she'll marry me this spring if we can work things out with farm jobs around here." With that he hurried up the remainder of the stairs and disappeared into his apartment.

"Well, at least there is some good news in all this miserable season," Whitedeer observed.

The two men began the long trek back to town and Strickland picked up where his deputy had left off. "Is it getting too much for you?" he asked. "I mean do you think you and Paula need to get away for a bit too?"

Charles shook his head. "I just want it over," he said. "I want to think that we can somehow get our lives back to normal some day."

When the two men had returned, Charles followed the sheriff back to his office. "Now where can we go with this investigation?" he asked.

"I guess we'll go gun checking," Red said with a sigh. At that moment, the phone shrilled. "Sheriff Strickland," Red answered, sitting on the edge the desk.

"Sheriff, this is Sergeant John Stokes from the St Paul P. D. Your secretary called yesterday wanting to know some information about a Lynn Christman?"

"That's right," Red said, pulling the yellow legal pad to him. "Sorry to bother you on Christmas Eve."

"No trouble, had to be here anyway," the man on the other end said. "I have some information you might be interested in."

After a few minutes listening, Sheriff Strickland hung up the phone, jumped to his feet and grabbed his coat. "Come with me!"

IV

Penny and Paula had nearly finished delivering the gaily-wrapped packages of home-make cookies and fruit cakes. "Who've we got left," Paula asked.

"Miss Christman," Penny said.

"Well, at least we have made it seem a little more like Christmas for some poor people today," Paula said, guiding the car to a stop in front of the teacher's house.

"I still feel a little funny about this," Penny said, carefully sliding out of the car. She opened the back door and took out the last two tins holding a fruitcake and cookies. One tin showed a smiling Santa face, the other, a decorated Christmas tree.

"Your dad's right," Paula said, walking around the car to join her friend and taking one of the tins from her. "We're just being nice. We're both good students and I think she knows we aren't trying for any special grade consideration." The two girls walked carefully up the sidewalk to the front porch, where Penny rang the bell and they waited.

He twitched the drapes aside to make a crack through which he could peer out the living room window, and saw the two girls standing on the tiny front porch. He knew if he remained silent, they would go away in a few minutes. But then, on the other hand, he could invite them in.

One of them was that Strickland brat. She had missed the hay ride. What had her old man done after his parents were burned to death and he and Donna Lynn spent those agonizing months in the hospital? Nothing . . . nothing at all. A bad thing, the deputies had said. Things happen in the heat of a strike. Never find the culprits, they had said, but he knew who they were. They were the high school boys and their older brothers, sons of the stupid coal miners who had wanted his dad to be run out of town on a rail. Wasn't that what they had said? If it hadn't been for their dad, they could have gotten their demands met by the head of the company. But no, his dad felt things could be settled to the benefit of the mine and the company. Really, in a way, his father had gotten what he deserved. The stupid bastard had cared more about saving his company some money than he did about his family. Well, then he was dead, and Mom was dead and then the strike had stopped. He smiled. Well, in a way the old fool had got what he wanted. He'd saved the company lots of money on the strike and then the company had to pay it out on all those medical bills. But now he'd gotten even for the deaths, for the pain, and for his horrible disfigurement. Now he might as well finish the getting even.

He looked at the girls standing on the porch. Friday night had been so easy. The kids, those stupid kids, caroling all over town. Lynn had offered them hot chocolate; he had slipped in the drugs. Maybe another cup of chocolate? Maybe this time he would let them stay awake, like Betsy, stupid, fat Betsy Klein. He knew all about how she had brought her little stories to Lynn. She knew a secret about someone, Betsy had confided to the teacher, a terrible secret that if anyone knew, they would know who had killed the kids Friday night. What should she do?

He couldn't let Betsy tell the story about him and his sister. They would know. They would suspect the truth, if they knew about Donna Lynn and Donald Lawrence Owens, sharing a home, a life, and their love. They would find out that Lynn Christman wasn't Lynn Christman at all but rather the girl they hadn't given a damn about all those years ago.

Betsy had been shocked to wake up in his company. She was disbelieving at first. Imagine, she thought he was Lynn. How stupid! It was true, they were twins, but still after the fire, and the scars, how could anyone mistake him for beautiful, unscarred Lynn?

Cutting out her tongue had been such an inspiration. He couldn't remember exactly from where that idea had sprung, perhaps an old Tom Tryon book, at any rate, it was sheer inspiration. By the time Betsy had died, his feeling of power, his sexual arousal, had been almost more than he could stand. He had wanted Lynn then, needed her more than ever before. He guessed tonight, after everyone was asleep, he would probably have to do a better job of cleaning up Lynn's basement where Betsy had died, and he would have to get rid of the damning evidence Lynn had found in the closet. But then what? He went to answer the doorbell which one of the girls had rung a second time.

"Hi, Miss Christman," Penny said, as the front door was opened. "Paula and I thought you'd like these cookies and the fruit cake we've brought."

"Come in, girls," he said. "Thanks so much for thinking of Lynn. I'm sorry she isn't here right now."

Penny and Paula exchanged looks and stared at Lynn Christman. She was wearing brown slacks and a tan sports shirt, open at the neck. Her brown eyes were strange, glittering. She spoke in a voice deepened an octave from its usual, pleasing contralto. They had stepped a short way into the living room as Penny offered the tin she had been holding. Now they exchanged startled glances as Miss Christman stepped around them and deliberately slid home the deadbolt.

"We really can't stay long," Paula stammered. "We've got other deliveries to make."

"Oh, but you'll have to stay for awhile," Lynn Christman, who somehow wasn't Lynn Christman, said smoothly. "Just sit down over there." As she spoke, she grasped each of the girls by an arm and propelled them to the couch. "We'll have a nice little visit."

"My dad knows I was coming here," Penny said, her face pale and her eyes now very round and frightened.

Lynn Christman took the tins of cookies and fruit cake from the two girls and set them on an end table. "Please let me introduce myself. I'm Donald Lawrence Owens, better known as Larry. I'm Lynn's twin brother."

Penny looked helplessly at Paula who was staring in disbelief. "Miss Christman?" she said shakily. "I don't understand."

Penny got to her feet and pulled Paula up with her. "We've really got to go," she said, trying to keep her voice level and edging toward the door.

"Oh, you can't go just yet," Lynn said. "You've got to help me with a little experiment."

Paula had edged toward the end of the couch. She wasn't sure just what action she wanted to take, but she hoped she could perhaps make a run for the back door while Miss Christman--Donald Owens--was talking to Penny.

"Stop right there, Paula!" The voice was sharp and commanding. "You don't want to leave good company. Besides, you wouldn't want to leave your friend here alone with me, now would you?"

Paula sank back into the cushions and shook her head. "No," she whispered. "I guess not."

I want both of you girls to listen carefully, very carefully." Lynn said and, reaching into her pants pocket, she pulled out a small gun. "Paula, I want you to walk very slowly to the door, unbolt it and open it. I have the barrel of my gun right against the back of Penny's head. The three of us are going to take a little ride."

"Do what she says," Penny whispered, "she's not kidding!"

Paula walked slowly and carefully to the door, unlocked it and slowly opened it. She thought maybe she could see someone outside and shout for help but there was no one in sight. She turned back toward the room to find out Christman had pushed Penny right up to the doorsill, leaving her with nothing more to do than lead the way outside. The little procession walked slowly from the house to the car parked in front.

"Get in behind the wheel, Paula," the Miss Christman thing ordered. "Sit with your hands in plain sight on the wheel and don't do anything else until I tell you."

As Paula was obeying the order, Christman shepherded Penny around the car and ordered her to sit in the front passenger seat. "I'm going to be sitting right behind you," she said, closing the car's front door and sliding into the rear seat behind Penny. "You see why I didn't want you to start the car before now, don't you?" she said to Paula, settling herself with the gun resting on Penny's left shoulder, pointed directly into her left ear. "Now, Paula, drive to the school."

Paula looked at her friend and then started the car. She wondered about speeding up very fast and then slamming on the brakes. Would that distract this crazy woman or would she shoot Penny the instant she suspected what Paula had in mind. That was a dumb thought! She knew she couldn't take the chance. She concentrated on driving slowly and carefully up the street toward the school. When the car reached the school parking lot, Lynn Christman, again with the gun pressed tightly to the back of Penny's head, directed Paula to lead the way to the door.

Although the walk had been shoveled since the last snowfall there were still icy patches and as the Christman thing tried to hurry the girls along, Penny slipped and fell to the cement walk. "If you're trying to delay things," Christman said, jerking her painfully to her feet, "it isn't going to work."

"I can't go fast," Penny stammered through chattering teeth. "I'm sorry but this cast…"

Christman smiled grimly as she pushed Penny roughly before her. "Oh you won't have to worry about the cast for much longer, Penny," she hissed.

When the three of them stood huddled in the portico, Christman handed her keys to Paula and directed her to open the door. "Obviously Penny can't move as quickly as you can," she said. "So if you decide to try something now, she'll be on your conscience."

"It won't matter anyway," Paula shot over her shoulder as she pushed open the heavy door that would admit them into the main floor of the school. "You'll kill us anyway."

"There's always a chance I won't," Christman mocked. "You might be smarter than your friends were. At least Lynn's always given you credit for being smarter." She pulled the heavy outer door closed, and the three of them proceeded into the main hallway and then down the stairs to the girls' locker room.

"Take off your coat," Christman ordered the startled girl. "You take off your coat, too, Penny, and your blouses. Now Paula, tie Penny's hands behind her back with your blouse; and," the menace in her voice was clear, "don't try to be cute. I'll check the knots."

When Paula had obeyed, the teacher asked her to put her own hands behind her back and she tied them securely with Penny's blouse. "I have to leave you for a little while," she said, and chuckled at the look the two girls exchanged, "Lie down on your stomachs," she ordered.

Paula complied at once, but Penny found the order difficult to obey because of the restricted movement of her leg. Christman grasped the girl roughly by the arm and threw her to the floor. Then she removed the slacks which each girl wore and bound their feet securely.

"Why are you doing this to us?" Paula cried as she heard the English teacher walk toward the door. But the door closed, her question unanswered.

Red Strickland, with a startled Charles Whitedeer following close behind, raced to the police car and slid into the driver's seat. The car was started and in motion almost before Charles could slide in and close the passenger door. "What's up?" he asked shakily.

"We're going to Lynn Christman's," Red said and didn't speak again until the car pulled up in front of the Christman house with a shriek of brakes.

The two men jumped from the car and raced to the door which, to Red's surprise, he found unlocked. In the living room, the two men's attention was caught immediately by the two tins which lay on the end table. "You take this floor," Red ordered, pulling his gun, "I'm going to the basement."

In a very few minutes the two men returned to the living room. "I even checked the garage," Red said. "Her car's here. I hate to take the time, but get on the phone and rouse all the deputies. I want this town searched from top to bottom."

VI

Penny had never known the school building to be so quiet. True the huge furnace was in operation but turned low, to keep the plumbing from freezing, but aside from its occasional hiss, and the popping and creaking normal to an old building, the school was completely still. "Where do you think she's gone now?" she whispered.

"Not far enough," Paula said softly. "I don't think she just tied us up so she could make the great escape."

"You know something funny," Penny said, trying to wriggle into a more comfortable position. "I know it's Miss Christman, but somehow it isn't Miss Christman. Does that make sense?"

Paula nodded. "It's the eyes and the mouth," she said. "The eyes don't belong . . . are strange."

"Do you think we could risk screaming?" Penny asked.

"I'd try if I knew where she was," Paula said, "but we're not even sure she's gone. I think she'll kill us."

"She's going to kill us anyway," Penny said. "Let's try."

Before the two girls could carry out their plan, the door to the locker room opened and Lynn Christman re-appeared. Penny went numb when she saw what the teacher had in her hands.

"I've been to the wood shop," Christman announced. "They keep nice, sharp tools there. Oh yes, girls, I've also moved your car."

The teacher bent to untie the feet of the girls as she spoke. "I've really nothing against you, Paula. You weren't here when Bannah killed our parents and left me so scarred for the rest of my life." As she spoke and after she had finished untying Penny's feet, she gave both frightened girls a sharp jerk upward. "But you . . ." she said, turning Penny to face her. "Your dad didn't do a thing to find out who started the fire. It was all too bad, according to him, but those things just happen at the time of a strike, you know."

"I wasn't even born then," Penny said, staring into the eyes she had always thought so kind and compassionate. Those eyes were now glittering with insane rage and hate.

"We're going to go into the showers," Christman ordered. "It's easier to clean up afterwards . . ."

VII

Red and Charles were now coordinating a search of the town with the other officers, using the car's radio. Red had hurriedly issued orders for the search by using the telephone at Christman's house. "Bannah's not that big," Red said, turning down yet another side street. "They've got to be in your car."

"I don't know what you got on the phone," Charles said, "but I found the clothes, including the brown jacket in the back of the closet of the second bedroom."

Red's face was pale, his mouth set in a straight, white line. "There's blood in the basement," he said through clenched teeth. "Christman tried to clean it up but there's more than enough for us to get a blood match with Betsy. We've got to find them," he said, skidding around the corner and then slamming on his brakes. Paula's car sat in front of his own house. "Maybe it's all right," he said, jumping from the car and racing for his door. But except for the startled cat, the house was empty.

As they started back for Red's car, a breathless Kathryn Nye intercepted them. "There's something funny going on, Red," she panted. "I came to see if there was anything I could help the girls with for tomorrow's dinner and saw Miss Christman pull Paula's car to the curb."

"Where did she go?" Red demanded, knowing that he didn't even sound civil.

"I don't know," Kathryn admitted. "She began walking north. But Red, as cold as it is outside, she wasn't even wearing a jacket and she just had some kind of house slippers on her feet."

"Thanks," Red called back to her as he jumped into the car. "I'm sorry but I'll explain all this later." Charles ran back from looking into his car and climbed in the other side of the patrol car. He had something clutched in his hand.

VIII

The two girls stood side by side in one of the large showers in the shower room with their faces to the wall, hands still bound behind their backs.

"It's too bad," Christman commented in the strange, low voice she was using, "that Lynn and I will have to leave Bannah after this . . . she didn't really want this, you know . . . but then Lynn's always been soft. She was willing to forget the past. But then she didn't suffer quite in the same way I did."

"No, actually I don't know, " Penny said, and turned to face Christman. She was stalling for time. Maybe something would happen. Surely her father realized they were missing and would come. Someone might come down for whatever reason, maintenance or she didn't know what, but there had to be a way. "Why was that?"

"Lynn wasn't burned as badly as I was." Christman continued. "They said I was burned over eighty-five percent of my body. They said I couldn't live." The mad woman gave a horrible giggle. "But I did, you know. Lynn kept me alive . . . kept our love alive. She loved me despite all my scars . . . and I protected her, just like I'm protecting her now."

By this time Paula had also turned to face the teacher, and the two girls exchanged a look. The smooth, slightly lined, every-day, familiar face of Miss Lynn Christman, their English teacher, stared back at them. There were no scars, and she was no man. But those eyes . . . oh God . . . those mad eyes!

"But you aren't burned!" Paula whispered. "Who are you anyway?"

The woman they had known for two years as Lynn Christman gave a throaty laugh. "Lying to me won't do you any good," she said opening her shirt and revealing nearly perfect skin with only a few faint scars between the area of her breasts and the waistband of her slacks. *"Look at me!"* she shrieked. *"My face, my hands, my body, all burned! All scarred! Who but Lynn could even look at me without getting sick?"*

The girls stared uncomprehendingly. "Who are you?" Penny whispered, still not understanding.

"I'm Donald Owens," the Lynn Christman thing said, voice deep and now eerily quiet. "Your father, Miss Strickland, had the opportunity to prevent a terrible thing from happening. The people of your wonderful little town poured gasoline around my parents' house and set fire to it. My sister, Donna Lynn, risked her life to drag me out before I burned to death. I promised myself one day I'd pay all of you people back."

The two girls stood in stunned silence. Miss Christman, Lynn Christman, Donna Lynn Owens? It was all too confusing. Here stood a woman with minimal burn scars believing she was a totally disfigured man!

"Well, we've talked enough," Lynn said. "It's time to finish this." She took the sharp keyhole saw she had been idly swinging in her hand and reached for Penny's long, red-blond hair. Pulling her head back sharply she exposed the frightened girl's throat.

Then everything seemed to happen at once. Penny screamed; Paula threw herself at the Lynn Christman *thing*. The school bell, left on over the holidays, shrilled, and Red and Charles burst into the shower room.

EPILOGUE

Penny and Red sat on the large couch in the Strickland living room, where the lights from the Christmas tree twinkled off and on merrily. Boots, the cat, lay in Penny's lap and she absently stroked his thick fur. Close to Red on the other side of the couch sat Katherine Nye. Across the coffee table from them on the loveseat were Charles and his sister.

"We'll put you on the force," Red said to Paula who sat with a glass of brandy in her hand. "You did some mighty quick thinking."

"I hoped Miss Christman wouldn't see me when I left my *BANNAH SCHOOL DAYS* notebook on the seat. I'd slid it from my purse when she first made me get into the car, and dropped it when we were leaving it. I hoped you, or someone, would see it."

"I wonder if she'd have shot me right in front of the school if she'd seen it," Penny said, picking up her own glass of brandy and taking a sip. "You know, when she held that saw to my throat, I could see all my life passing before me, just like they say in the movies!"

"I thought that only happened when you were drowning," Charles said, smiling in appreciation of her little joke. The girls were remarkably recovered and calm considering what had happened to them.

"Let's hope, Kitten," her father commented, getting up to add more logs to the cheerfully crackling fire, "that by the next time your life passes before you there will be a lot more of it to pass."

"I still don't understand, Daddy," Penny said. "It *was* Miss Christman, wasn't it?"

"It was and it wasn't," Red said, settling himself back into a comfortable position. "It all started a long time ago, when I first ran for sheriff, as a matter of fact. She and her brother lived here back in the 60's." He proceeded to outline the events of the strike and the subsequent fire that had killed the parents and had put the twins in the Burn Center in Minneapolis.

"Donald was burned so badly there was no way he could live," Red continued, sipping at his own drink and then setting it on the table beside him and selecting one of the cookies sitting on a colorful holiday plate on the low table between the couch and chairs. "Lynn tried to go back into the bedroom to rescue him, but was overcome by smoke. She was the first one found and really had suffered very little in the way of physical injury. But she remained in the hospital long after her brother had died because of the severe psychological trauma she suffered." He washed down a bit of cookie with another sip of his drink and continued. "Apparently the doctors thought the shock was due to the loss of her family. They didn't know the whole story."

"What was that?" Kathryn asked, looking over at him interestedly.

"We found stacks of journals in the closet of the spare bedroom of her house," Red began. "From what I can gather, Lynn and her brother had been . . . well . . . more than a brother and sister should be to each other for a long time before the fire. I think Lynn blamed herself for not being as badly hurt as he was. She was in a different part of the house when it caught on fire but the gasoline spread around the house by the perpetrators caused the fire to start in Donald's room. She called the fire station from the kitchen and then went back for Donald. That was why she was able to escape relatively unharmed."

"Donald really died then?" Penny asked, leaning forward.

"Yes, not long after that," Red continued. "Lynn couldn't accept that. She needed him to be alive. She needed him to still love her. She kept the journals and agonized over what happened in their past and now in their present. She knew deep down that Donald/Larry, or at least the part of her that became her brother in times of stress, had done these killings but she simply couldn't face it."

"And because of something that happened all those years ago, my Marcia and all those other children died?" Kathryn demanded, wiping the tears that had begun to slide down her cheeks.

"I'm afraid so," Strickland said, sliding a comforting arm around her shoulders. "I blame myself for not having checked up on her background sooner, but she seemed so . . ."

"So normal?" Kathryn said.

"There's no doubt about who killed everyone," Charles put in. "The basement looked like...well let's just say that while Christman did a fair job of cleaning up Betsy's blood, there was a lot she missed. I'll also wager next year's pay that the fiber the crime lab found in that boot print will match the carpet in Christman's living room." Then turning to the sheriff he added, "By the way, you never did tell me what the phone call from St. Paul was about?"

Red sighed. "A lot of pretty bad things happened to Lynn over the years following the fire here. Her uncle was sexually abusing her after her aunt died. Lynn escaped in the only way she knew how. Donald had to save her, to protect her. After all, Donald loved her and he was the only person she wanted in her bed."

"But that's sick," Penny blurted.

"Lynn was pretty messed up mentally by that time," Red agreed. "From the ramblings in her journals it was obvious she had pulled herself into her own world, a world where she and Donald were safe, happy, and still needed only each other. Then her uncle was killed, brutally bludgeoned to death. The police had their suspicions that Lynn might have been somehow involved. There was no sign of forcible entry; but she made it sound so convincing, and she was, after all, only a teenager that they finally believed her."

"She actually killed her uncle?" Paula breathed.

"Oh yes," Red said, stroking Kathryn's hair as he continued his narrative. "Then she went on to college and got romantically involved with a boy. They were to be married. He died the night of their graduation. Lynn said a stranger had attacked them while they were parked. She had run away, had suffered a broken—well, it turned out to be really only a sprained—ankle while getting away."

"Donald ... or rather Lynn, killed him too?" Paula asked.

"That's right."

"But why the kids at school?" Penny demanded, getting to her feet and going to look out the window. "We didn't do anything to her."

"Lynn/Donald believed that the parents of the kids in her class were directly responsible for the fire that killed their parents. As Donald, she couldn't bear the fact that those men had gone on to have families, lead normal lives, and go unpunished. And I think probably more than anyone else in this town she hated me. "

"But were they actually involved?" Charles asked.

"Some of them may have been," Red admitted. "It would have been a hard thing to prove. There were lots of outside agitators here during that time. There was no proof one way or the other."

"What will happen to her?" Paula asked, making room for the cat who had been unceremoniously dumped to the floor when Penny had gone to stare out the window.

"She'll be put away, evaluated and treated."

"Will she ever come to trial?" Katheryn wondered.

"Maybe some day, when she can accept the fact that she really was responsible for all the deaths."

"What about Sam Tuttle?" Charles asked.

"We might never know exactly," Red admitted, "but that little .22 that she held on you girls was the gun that killed Sam."

"It was clever of her to put Betsy's keys in Sam's pocket after she killed him," Charles observed.

Red nodded. "Yes. If the fire had truly done its job and Sam's body had been more badly burned she might have gotten away with that one."

"Was that in her journal too?" Kathryn asked.

"Red nodded. "Sam invited her up to talk about Betsy. Remember, I mentioned to her that Sam said he had called her. She denied that call. Now I think Sam really made it. She went up there to see how much he knew."

"Why kill him?" Charles pursued.

"From the way she was when Penny and Paula got to the house, I think the Donald/Larry part of Lynn was making itself stronger and more dominant. As she committed these hideous crimes, she more and more was unable to face the situation as Lynn. So Donald became stronger and stronger. Maybe he emerged at Sam's house, just like he did when the girls arrived at her house with those presents; as I said, we may never know."

"But how did she keep up the illusion that he was there, Daddy?" Penny asked, resuming her seat.

"She talked to him, called on him, probably masturbated to relieve her sexual frustrations. She even had a room and closet with the clothes, in her sizes, that 'Donald' wore. He just became more and more the dominant of the two personalities. I don't believe Lynn knew that first morning when I interviewed her, that she had been responsible for the death of those kids. Up to that time, she had been able to call Donald when she needed him, after that night, or perhaps during the time the kids came to her house, Donald had become the stronger, for a little while at least. Then when Betsy Klein came over to share her story, not dreaming the horrible secrets Lynn had to hide, enter Donald to the rescue. From her really disjointed journal entries following Betsy's visit, Lynn/Donald thought the jig was up. He thought somehow Betsy had discovered the secret of Lynn and himself when in reality Betsy was only talking about the secrets of the Movieland rentals."

"That's so terrible!" Penny exclaimed. "Poor Betsy, always trying to make points with Miss Christman and to think all it got her was killed!"

Red got to his feet and refilled their empty brandy glasses. "So much hate boiling over in one person," he said, settling himself back down beside Kathryn and taking her hand.

"Maybe that wasn't all there was to it," Charles observed, cupping the brandy snifter in his big hands. "She was finding some kind of acceptance here, maybe more affection from the kids. Maybe the Donald part of her finally felt his hold was slipping a little. Maybe it was jealousy, too, that made him kill those kids."

"You're in the wrong field, Charles," Red observed. "Maybe you should go back to school and get into psychology or something."

"I think I'll leave that kind of thing to people who can deal with it a lot better than I can," Charles grinned.

The big mantle clock began its sonorous chiming of midnight. Red stood, and motioning to the others to do the same, raised his glass. "Merry Christmas, and may we finally truly be blessed with peace on earth and even more so peace in our hearts and our town!"

THE END

good C- 1-05

9 781933 037264